WATER FOR BLOOD

A TWISTING WORLD TALE

ALEA HENLE

CRABGRASS
PUBLISHING

CONTENT WARNING

This novel includes evil done to a child.

THE ZOO

Grampa had two goals the summer I turned eighteen. After all, he had only a little while longer to live—though he never came right out and said he was dying, but why else would he want to drag me on a quest for the conquistador who'd stolen the fountain of youth centuries ago. He didn't tell me the second goal until much later: to make me cry.

For some reason, we started the quest with a visit to the Philadelphia Zoo, accompanied by my little brother, Louie, who still didn't understand Grampa and I were leaving the next day.

Louie rocked blue shorts and his favorite shirt, a Jolly Quakers batball jersey in black-gray-black-yellow stripes. I matched him down to scuffed walking shoes, except I used a length of yellow ribbon to tie back my hair while he clapped on a batball hat. Him big for six and me short, flat, and undergrown, and both of us in matching colors would make it easier to find him if he got lost.

He jammed his hands into his pockets, stuck his feet into his battered shoes, and slumped as he thumped his way along. I followed, sweltering under the morning haze. Brick houses lined the street, still begrimed despite last night's late spring rain. Puddles steamed on the pavement alongside empty beer bottles, burger wrappers, and half-gnawed wing bones. Someone—maybe the college kids who stomped around the apartment above—had had quite the party and whirled themselves down the block flinging sweet potato fries all around.

Grampa managed to appear dapper enough his shadow should step out and dance with him. His yellow shirt buttoned down and he'd rolled the long sleeves up. White hair with a touch of gray showed beneath a black felt hat with a broad brim. His dark brown eyes, steep nose, and slow smile twisting to the left—so much like my dad's that goose-bumps lined my arms.

His zig-zag walking stick had a sharp metal tip which glittered in the light every time he stabbed a torn bag of food. He swiveled and dislodged the trash with a flick of his wrist. It landed atop an overflowing bin, but stuck rather than rolling back off. All along the walk up the long block to the tram station, he stabbed wing bones and wrappers, dumping them but not saying anything.

We caught the flex tram at the intersection. The long, serpentine sections hissed to a stop and Louie bounded on. Grampa had tight hold of his cane, but offered me a hand to help board with the other. I hung back. Shouldn't it be me helping him up, given his condition and all? He shrugged and boarded, slipping the driver coins to cover our fares, and I slunk along behind.

The zoo lay far enough out of the city that we crossed a couple of parks and untenanted places. Louie loved sitting backwards on the seat watching the rails extend and retract as we rode along. He smashed his nose hard against the glass the whole way. The air conditioning kept things cool and dust out, though it had a swampy taste which left a sour residue in my mouth.

At least it didn't trigger my brother's allergies.

The zoo did.

We'd never had pets, and I'd never been sick a day in my life, so somehow no one considered the problem of exposing Louie to a lot of really big, really cool, and ready-to-shed cats. We could've made it through without too much trouble if Louie'd only stayed far enough back from fences rather than hanging over them when the wind blew up bits of dust and hair. As well tell rain not to fall.

"Wow, check out this monkey here or hey look at the hippo!" I said, each time he gave the faintest whistle on his breath. Grampa strolled along behind, swinging his cane now and then.

Louie liked everything, but nothing caught his attention for long. It was hello-cool-neat-what's next . . . until he noticed the big cats wandering across mesh-wrapped bridges above our heads and tried to find the best place to get close to them.

The first whiff of cat hair didn't do much, but within a few more breaths he went into full-on wheeze. I stuffed the inhaler in his hand—glad Mom insisted I take it—and dragged him away.

Wheeze and heave, he drew in the meds and glared at me. Soon as his breathing cleared, he squirmed and tried to run back. I set my back against a warm stone wall for balance. Wrapping my arms around him, I pinned him no matter how he wriggled. My fingers pressed against his shoulders, trying to ease their tightness.

"Wanna see the cats!"

"How about . . ." I flailed, searching for any sign of inter-esting-to-a-six-year-old-boy animals nearby. "A swan? Or a goat?"

"Cats!" Louie kicked.

The rough sole of his shoe scraped across my shin. I bit back a snarl.

"Why?"

"'Cause, they're big with claws and fangs."

Before I could answer, Grampa caught up with us. He struck his cane against the wall with a rattling thud.

"Mmph. You want big? Try an alligator, my boy." He tucked his cane under one arm and put his wrists together. His fingers wiggled, then he slapped his palms. Louie and I both jerked. "Big mouth, big teeth, the better to bite you."

"Really big?"

"Oh, the biggest. Somewhere out there lies the snarliest gator you ever might see, with such a wide mouth you could crawl in and hide." Grampa framed his face with his open hands on either side, fingers clawed. "Unless he chooses to close his mouth and swallow you down. Gulp!"

"Where's a gator?" Louie twisted his head around. "Mara, gator time!"

"This-a-way," Grampa grabbed Louie's hand and led him along a short walk into the wide, dark maw of the reptile house.

Inside smelled antiseptic instead of dank, marshy, swamp. My arms clenched tight against my sides as I passed snakes slithering among branches, but surely the air in here beat cat fur flying.

Louie darted from one viewing station to another. One moment he peered up at a brown and tan lizard seemingly made of hundreds of miniature beads stuck together. A few minutes later, he dashed over and around to press his face against glass as a pig-nosed turtle swam by. A second turtle, with a different nose, flapped its limbs and floated along. Between the two, they kept him entertained for longer than most.

With soft thumps of metal hitting concrete, Grampa tromped over. His arm brushed mine. I sidled over a step to leave room for cool air-conditioning to blow between us.

"Hmph." He clapped his cane down before him. His fingers rapped on the polished head.

Over along the far wall, Louie waved a hand at the turtles.

"The zoo wasn't the best of choices for him." Grampa heaved a sigh.

"He's having fun." So I should've suggested something else? Who was he to tell me? He'd visited twice a year, a few days each time, but we never went anywhere much. Mostly hung out at home or his hotel room, or went for walks around the neighborhood.

"He is, indeed. I mean no insult. It is on me, not to have asked or thought." More rapping of fingers against the wood. "I remember him coughing, but not so long and hard."

Silence grew between us, chill as the breeze from a nearby vent. I shifted back and forth, scuffing my shoes against the floor.

"It's getting worse. You wouldn't know if you weren't here." I risked turning my head a tad. His shoulders had slumped a little.

"And if you saw no reason to tell me."

"Why would you care? He's not your relation."

"You are my granddaughter. He is your brother." Grampa clomped around to stand in front of me. He stood only a couple of inches taller, making his gaze hard to avoid. "That makes him my grandson."

"Yeah. Right." Nice thought, and yeah Grampa'd always been kind to Louie. Brought him gifts every visit, and no fewer or lesser quality than me. Bought his ticket today, along with mine.

"Why not believe me?"

"When you showed up, after Dad died, you had a paternity test in hand."

"The results, yes. We found them among some belongings your father left in storage." Grampa lifted a steady hand to tuck stray hairs behind my ear, quick and soft as a breeze. "I didn't know you existed until then, or I'd have come to visit before."

"Sure."

He didn't say as much, never had, but his interest hinged on me being Dad's daughter. Blood mattered to Grampa. A lot. And to Dad. I hadn't known about the test until Grampa's arrival. Mom put the best spin on it she could, when I finally figured it out—telling me Dad doubted her—but I couldn't ask Dad why, and Grampa didn't answer, just laid down some nonsense about me understanding when I was older.

Grampa hiked off to join Louie by the turtles. He pulled a flask out of his shirt pocket. The bright brass trim glittered in the light. Soon as his hands started working off the cap, I zoomed right over and nabbed it before he could pass it down to Louie.

"It's water, from home." Grampa smiled down at my brother.

"May I?" I waited for his permission, though I'd have gone ahead without it. Dad had a flask almost exactly like this, maybe a bit more beat up, and he never put water in it—not that he'd ever offered it to me, either. The first sniff didn't find anything, but on the second I got a faint whiff of something light and floral. When I tilted the flask back and let a few drops roll down my throat, I didn't taste anything but my own worry. "Thanks."

Louie grabbed it from my hands as I lowered it down and then took a big gulp.

"Go ahead and finish it off. There's more where that came from." Grampa patted him on the back, not looking at me.

A few drops dribbled out the edges of Louie's mouth, but he slurped it all down and gave a big burp. Passing the flask back to Grampa, he didn't say thank you until he caught my eye. Turning on a squeaky heel, he squealed and darted down the hall.

Next stop: the alligators. Or alligator, because I only saw one but it was more than enough all of itself.

A long black scaly body lay half in and half out of the water. The length alone stunned me, more than two meters long. The underside of the gator's massive jaw was beige, mostly matching the rocks on which it lay. All the rest gleamed in dark scales. It yawned, revealing a pink mouth filled with bright white teeth.

Louie leaned against the protective metal railing, pointing and counting the beast's teeth.

I gripped his soft shirt as he turned from side to side in search of uncounted teeth. Grampa stood on Louie's far side.

The alligator stirred, yawning wide and sending ripples through the water. Louie shrieked and went wild, and even I caught the teeth-counting fever because the long mouth contained so many sharp, white triangles.

"Do it again, do it again." Louie jumped up and down, hands drumming on the railing.

I twisted my hand tighter in his shirt, just in case, though it wasn't likely to do any good.

An odd sound, half-purr and half-chomp, flashed through me and made goosebumps appear all along my arms. It repeated a moment later—from *Grampa*.

His fingers wrapped tight around his cane as his chest and head stretched and contorted into odd positions. Neck tilted to one side and shoulder raised, he gave a third purr-chomp. His chest puffed out and head fell back as he burbled. Head down, shoulders hunched, and tongue twisting, he produced rippling trills.

The gator's tail lashed. It let out a roar that boomed and echoed until I dropped hold of Louie's shirt to cup my hands over my ears and try to stop the ringing. Louie buried his face against me, arms wrapped over his head. Around us, other spectators also cringed and covered their ears—except for Grampa.

He gave a chumpfing sound. A rill of vibrations rippled along my spine and arms, making me shiver.

The gator lumbered out of the water, tail still lashing. Turning in a half-circle, the beast lay down on the stone with its back to us. The tail tip twitched, then lay flat.

"Hmph." Grampa rolled his shoulders and shook his head.

"Were you," no one lurked near us, but I whispered anyway, "were you talking to it?"

"Wait, Grampa talked to the gator?" Louie wiggled out of my grasp to hang on Grampa's arm and cane. "Wicked cool! What'd he say? Was he yelling at you? How'd you learn to talk to gators?"

"And why?"

"You could learn." Grampa's eyes flicked my way, but he smiled down at Louie. "It takes years, though, and you'll need energy. How about lunch and perhaps, if you eat your greens, I'll tell you a story."

"How you learned to talk to gators?"

He put an arm around Louie and led him towards the exit. I lingered behind, watching the gator. The beast must've been listening or something, because it swung its head around and flicked its tail again before squirming into another position on the stone.

Walking outside the cool reptile house I slammed into a wall of heat. Wilting, I scanned the walks for Grampa and Louie. My brother jumped up and down, waving his arms, near a lush, open-air garden. Bright-colored umbrellas offered shade for a dozen or more tables.

Within moments, we had a seat under an umbrella. The server took our orders and left glasses of cool water with drops of condensation rolling down the sides. Louie drank and made a face.

"It doesn't taste as good as your water, Grampa."

"No." Grampa sipped his. "The ice is perhaps a tad stale, but it is well enough to parch a thirst."

"Blech," Louie opened his mouth to say more, but one look from Grampa and he subsided. Kicking his legs against the chair, he wiggled. "Story time?"

"I suppose."

"Not the gators." This had evidently been settled while I wasn't around. "How about the Spanish con thing you want Mara to kiss?"

Both Grampa and I blinked. I flushed and gritted my teeth while Grampa burst out laughing.

"No," he wiped a few tears from his eyes, "Conquistador means conqueror. I would never want Mara to kiss one."

"Even the guy who stole the fountain of youth?" I snorted. "Here I thought that was the plan. I'd kiss him while you got away with the fountain." In truth, I hadn't spent any time wondering what to do when we caught up with the conquistador because it was all a big hoax. Something for Grampa to fix on, maybe in hopes he'd get to drink from the fountain and get back his youth.

"No such plan." Grampa pointed at me with the sharptines end of a fork. "When we do find Eyague de—"

"Iago? Like in Othello?" I asked.

"No, Eyague." He scratched the name on the table with the fork. "Eyague de Torres. And when we find him, you stay well back, you hear? I won't have you lost to him."

"Not even for the fountain of youth?"

"It wasn't a fountain of youth." Grampa winced, mouth

wrinkling as though he'd sucked on a lemon rind too long. "Say, rather, a spring of life."

"What's the difference?" I asked.

"Fountain suggests shaping by human hand. Some mortal agency." Grampa shook his head. "What Eyague de Torres found on the hillside had nothing to do with humans, only divine nature."

"Okay." I shrugged. Louie looked bored, so I turned back to question burning me. "How do you steal a spring?"

"Did I never tell you the full story?"

The server came with our food before I could answer, but as soon as he'd gone, Grampa repeated the question.

"Tell me what? There was this guy who stole the fountain. You knew where he was once upon a time, but he got away." All the talk about eternity creeped me out. "You showed me a pair of old gloves once. Belonged to the conquistador? And somehow you'd gotten them but lost track of him."

"Is that all you remember?"

"Yeah." A sweet-vinegar smell distracted me as I dug into my salad. Lemon and peppers and greens filled my mouth.

"You never told me." Louie chomped his hamburger, half-mangling his words.

"It's not a tale for children, at the heart." Grampa scraped his fork across his plate, making almost as awful a sound as the alligator. "It's made of tangles and torture, blood and revenge, and evil done in the full light of day."

"Cool." Louie gave a thumbs up and grabbed a fry. "Tell!"

And so Grampa did.

THE SPRING OF LIFE

A very long time ago, many ages before I was born, no matter how old or young I seem to you, there lived in Spain a man named Eyague de Torres, of the towers, though he were better called d'amargura for he was a man of bitterness. All his family fell away from him, harrowed by the plague. Death became his constant companion, though it did not claim him, and hence Torres fixed on it as his bitterest enemy.

I tell you this not to arouse sympathy, but because even villains have their beginnings. Torres had no need to turn villain, though it is true he never considered himself such. He studied medicine, what his fellows knew of it, at least, which is far less than anyone does today. What he learnt might fit within your inhaler, young Louie, but he studied and meant well, that is to his credit. Too many of his patients, however, died. The more death followed upon Torres's heels, the more he searched for any way to foil it. Prayers, herbs, bitter draughts—and spellcraft.

His searches led him across the seas to New Spain, one of many looking for a new life in what seemed to them a new land.

I shall spare you the details about which you will not care. Let us settle this much: he joined the forces under Francisco Vázquez de

Coronado and ventured in search of fabled cities and gold. After a time, they made their way into lands which are now called the Pueblos Naciones.

To that point, so far as anyone else might care, Torres was but one of many. He wanted wealth as much as his compatriots, and listened to all tales of las Siete Ciudades de Cíbola. Yet more than all else he wished to live and deny death.

Which made him a dangerous man when he stumbled across a spring of life.

It was by the merest accident. Imagine, if you will, a group of men passing through wooded hills on an autumn day. Yellowing leaves flutter around, falling at the merest touch of a breeze. The sun, though, shines hot upon the men, who are garbed in heavy armor made of boiled leather and metal fixings.

They reach a spring trickling from the rocky hillside, flowing down through flowers and bushes. They are hot. Thirsty. They bend to drink.

Perhaps two or three take note of feathers and bright-colored stones laid beside the water's course. The soldiers, most poor, joke amongst themselves. They run their fingers through the smooth pebbles, discard the feathers, and scatter offerings as they quarrel over a fine piece of turquoise.

The strongest wins, the losers grow silent and sullen.

Refreshed, they pass on.

One notices the absence of aches and pains. The fading of scratches upon hands which had pushed through bushes. A new feeling of vitality running in his veins.

He alone ponders why and how sweet-scented flowers bloomed along the spring's banks though all the rest of the land and the plants rooted upon it had embraced autumn and bent towards winter.

He marks their passage away from the spring, so he may return.

For the spring, in its innocence, healed them as it healed all in pain who came to it. Beast or bird, bush or human, all were equal in its care and worthy of the power it bore. Born in fire and earth deep beneath a vast volcanic caldera, it knew only those humans who lived in nearby villages. They came bringing feathers and beads as gifts, and asked the favor of healing from the spring's waters. This it gave them—but it did the same for Torres and the other conquistadors.

And in healing him, gave him hope of earthly life everlasting.

It knew not what it wrought. Yet even had it known, it might not have restrained its healing, for that is what it was made to do . . .

"You talk as though the spring was alive and . . . could think." The blood in my veins grew chill at the idea of a conqueror bent on robbing a spring of life. A warm breeze wrapped around me, yet goose bumps covered my arms as the air seemed to whisper words in my ears. Conquista. Coronado. Cibola. Then, deeper, la vida eterna.

We'd finished eating and moved to a bench off the main path. Tree branches arched overhead, providing cool shade. Grampa sat at one end and me the other, with Louie sprawled between us. His head rested on my lap, a warm weight. Musky smells from the animals filled the air. One of the overhead paths for the cats to traipse along passed nearby, but so far Louie's breathing continued calm and even. He might've fallen asleep, for his eyes had closed.

"Why would you think it could not think?" Grampa tilted his head, silver flashing at his ears. "Is it not a living thing? Why would a spring of life not possess a spirit and sentience of its own?"

"I just thought—"

"Think again, and this time follow your thoughts all the way through to the end, no matter how strange and bitter, for that is likely to be the truth."

"Stop talking and get on with the story. It was getting good." Louie rolled over to lie on his side.

Grampa and I both laughed at the contradiction in Louie's order, but a frisson of tension remained between us.

Torres returned to the spring's banks, time after time.

On his first visit back, he cut himself as a test. The spring healed him. He'd brought a flask with him, similar to that which I carried today. Filling it, he took away waters with him.

Only to discover the healing power diluted with distance.

So back he came, as soon as ever he could. A third, fourth, fifth, twelfth time and always bringing more and varied vessels within which he sought to capture not merely the spring's water but its power.

Each time he failed. The water held virtue at the source, close by the spring, but the power dwindled when he stole it away. No material he could think of—clay, iron, silver, gold—could capture and keep both water and power.

It took him long, all winter and spring and into summer, but at length he realized that if he wanted the spring's healing power at his command, taking away water alone would not suffice. He could remain in these new lands and have access to the water. This he would not do. He despised the peoples and their ways of life. He longed to take power and water back across the seas to Spain.

To do this, he would have to reft the spring from the hillside.

He had to steal the spring of life.

Alas, he of all the men in Coronado's train had the means to discover a way to do so. Hidden among his bags were old grimoires, many steeped in evil. Torres devoted every spare moment to studying them. By the time Coronado turned for home, accepting he would not find in this land the treasures he sought, Torres had pieced together a desperate and despicable plan—to use the spring's own nature against it.

One day he rode out from camp, shortly before the last depar-

ture when all was chaos. This time, however, he headed along a canyon up into the wilderness.

There he lurked and waited near a village. Once many people lived there, filling wide-spread rooms and buildings. Most had left and moved down close to the great river. Only a few families remained, eking out their living as the wild encroached upon their homes and fields.

He watched long enough to spot what he sought: children going to a creek for water. Spurring his horse, he covered the distance and snatched at random. His choice fell on an unfortunate one, whom he carried off. A girl, younger than you Mara but older than Louie, whose cries resounded among the hills until he silenced her with a rag stuffed in her mouth.

Her people followed, but he expected as much. A tug at a leather tie on his saddle released a clay vessel. It fell and broke on hard-baked earth, loosing dust upon the wind. A magical dust which no breeze seemed able to resist blowing up into a miniature dust storm. He sacrificed this, one of his greatest treasures until he'd found the spring, so much did he wish to capture water and power. Between this and other stratagems, he escaped with the child. Bound her hands. Gagged her. Forced her to march with him to where the spring ran through the woods.

Now the spring knew nothing of this. It flowed, as always, until the day it felt the approach of Torres and the girl. She'd fought him until overpowered. Her pain flowed ahead. Her tears fell on the ground, agony seeping into the earth and reverberating far enough the spring awaited. Ready to ease her pain and heal her wounds.

Torres dumped the girl into the stream, face first, and held her head down.

Louie's soft snores whiffled along my legs, vibrating through my jeans. Grampa's voice dropped low, to a soothing sound that wouldn't rouse my brother—but didn't ease me at all. His dark eyes fixed on me. Although his words were spare and few, they grew in power as they combined in my head.

The story took me over, swallowed me down whole.

My mind divided into three parts. One listened to Grampa. At the same time, I quivered with the fear and rage and desperation of a child ripped from her home and drowning—alongside the surprise and intensity of a strange, alien intelligence bent on healing and preserving life.

Torres drowned the child. Air spirits whipped about him, plucking at his garments and tossing leaves, twigs, and pebbles into his face. He grunted and waved a hand before his eyes but kept at his purpose—and scattered precious herbs and leaves upon the water.

The spring lapped at the girl's body, filling her with warmth as it eased her aches and healed her. Pain rippled from child to spirit as the girl tried to hold her breath. She failed. Water seeped through, healing the damage even as drops slipped down her throat to her lungs.

She kicked out. Twice her size, he held fast with her legs pinned beneath him and both hands atop her head.

He drowned her again. Over and over, as the foliage he'd introduced into the water worked a perverse magic.

The spring held power for life, not death. Apart from a few lashes with waves crashing over the man, it brought all its powers, all its water, to bear on the child. Wrapped and soaked into the slender body, the spring sought to keep her whole and hale and living. Breezes tore about and air spirits called out, tugging at the spring, but its spirit paid no heed.

Even as the spring sought to preserve the girl's life, to heal the damage of being held under its waters, it was drawn drop by drop into the child's body.

Until it no more sprang forth from the earth. A harsh burst of pain hit not the girl, but the spring. All sense of the world drained away. The deep fire, the earth, it lost those and found nothing to hold instead. An odd, insistent beat drove the spring's waters through narrow channels which ran straight, then split and twisted only to gather and reform.

Imprisoned in human flesh, the spring became trapped in the cycle of blood, pumped from heart throughout the body only to return and be sent out again and again.

No more could the spring extend its awareness through the glade, or speak with the air spirits—now it was limited to eyes, ears, nose, mouth, and skin. When the girl opened her eyes on a drying landscape, the spring did not at first recognize its home in the track of mud trailing from the rocky hillside. Then it knew, but would not accept. It tried to return to the earth, but what does a spring, which flows over land, know of bodily movement? Of bones, muscles, and flesh?

It had no chance. Neither did the girl, who now shared her body with a spirit not of her choosing. The spring called to the girl, speaking to it as it would to the breezes and air spirits. The girl spoke in her language. Two spirits, human and water, trapped together in the one body and neither able to understand the other.

Torres pounced upon them. Drawing a knife, he slit her wrist. Water and blood flowed forth. Of these he drank and knew he had succeeded. Power and healing flowed in his veins. He carried the girl and the spring away with him, far from the mountains and hills. Each swore to find some way to return, even as he reft them from where they belonged.

And somewhere on this earth, he lives still.

Thank God Louie slept. Grampa shouldn't ever have told the story where he could've heard. The horror made my blood run cold and goosebumps cover my skin. I sniffed, sympathy for the girl and spring lingering in my bones, even though I wasn't all-the-way sure they'd existed. Grampa told a good tale, but I nothing I'd ever heard about magic worked that way. Especially since there wasn't much magic in the world way back then. All the magic gifts people had now days only dated back to 1815 and the eruption of Mount Tambora, according to all my teachers and just about every book I'd ever read.

Grampa reached over Louie's snoring body and touched the skin beneath my eyes on both sides. I flinched, drawing back. He frowned at his dry skin.

"No tears."

"I don't cry." I crossed my arms over my chest, rubbing my skin to warm it. Unfortunately, another sniff escaped me, but I found the hole in Grampa's logic and that heated me up. "How did you ever learn the story? And don't tell me you ran into Torres drunk in a bar and he confided in you."

"I won't because that isn't what happened. As far as I know, Torres never told anyone. But you need to remember" —he leaned forward and grabbed my cold hands in his warm ones—"he wasn't there alone. He had company in his victims, the child and the spirit of the spring. Plus spirits of the air and earth, the trees arching overhead, and the breezes blowing through them, witnessed it all."

"And they told you?"

"In point of fact, I first read it in a letter, many long years ago. Before your father's birth." He gave a wry chuckle. "Before I learned to speak with birds and alligators. You might say the second time I learned the tale, I heard it from a bird."

"What about birds?" Louie yawned and sat up, stretching. He burped, sharing the smell of half-digested burger. "Where're we going next?"

"Time to go home." I checked my watch, startled at the time. A glance overhead showed the sun well along its way.

"Yes, for tomorrow we leave." Grampa ruffled Louie's hair. "You'll miss Mara, I know, but I have need of her for a while, and then she will be back."

"So where are we going?" I frowned at him as I hugged

Louie close. He clutched at me, burying his head against my chest. Trust Grampa to hit on the hardest part of traveling with him.

"The gator was quite helpful, and said to go South or West."

"The gator said?"

"I asked him," Grampa said. "Alligators usually keep track of Torres, so talking to them will help us choose our way."

"Most of the country is South or West." Some help.

"Yes." Grampa nodded. "But at least now we know we needn't go to New York or New England."

DREAMS

Grampa's story snuck into my dreams that night. As I slipped into sleep, tiredness turned to complete and utter exhaustion. The muscles lining my legs jumped and jerked, my arms likewise. My weary feet prickled at the edge of numbness. Pain never fully set in, for even as I verged on agony, a sweet, soothing warmth flowed through me leaving ease in its wake.

Above all else, my heart beat loud and insistent: ka-thump, ka-thump.

My vision narrowed and doubled at one and the same time. I dreamed and knew myself dreaming as I trudged across an endless landscape of hard earth, pebbles, and scrub brush. Low hills and gullies made straight passage impossible. The sun shone hard on my bowed head and shoulders, heating the strange, broad-weave cloth covering me from neck to knee. Eyes low and shoulders hunched, I was one of a horde of walkers following footprints and hoofprints, while avoiding steaming piles of manure, pitted hollows that stank of urine, and the occasional dead horse.

Hot, dry air sucked moisture from my mouth, leaving

behind the taste of bitter dirt and blood. Metal clanged, marking where the strange pale men walked among us or rode high above. Laughter grated on my ears, along with strange phrases in tongues I didn't understand. Here and there, I recognized a word or two but no more.

Yet at the same time, I saw nothing, heard nothing, nor smelled nor tasted. The only world I knew was the rush of liquid through tunnels, narrow and wide. I pulsed with the flow of blood, ka-thump, ka-thump, dashing down arteries, channeling through capillaries, and then back into veins. Where pain existed, there I loosed my magic to offer ease.

Two spirits, one body. Separate, yet joined. Together—and alone.

As water, I ran in circles. Burbling. Rippling. Seeking to speak with spirits of the air or this flesh in which I was prisoned and wailing in grief and anger when they did not answer.

As a human girl, the warmth and healing in my blood made me quake. My body belonged to me, and yet did not, for the strangeness of another spirit existed within me. One who at any moment might jerk my limbs this way and send me reeling and forgetting how to walk for moments at a time.

As me, dreaming, I marked the strange flow of time in jerks and fits. The dream warped back and forth between slow and fast, but always kept me bouncing between those two vantage points.

Now and then one of the horde came close and tried to speak with me-as-girl. A tall man all in black. A warrior wearing turquoise beads. Once a soldier with a woman at his side who spoke words my dream self recognized, although I didn't know what she said.

Each time, my captor, stinking of hate and blood, arrived at my side. He kept an eye always on me and spoke to those who had approached me in his strange tongue. Often they nodded and walked away. A few times, he tossed herbs in the air. When they finished falling, we had moved or the others had, for the horde mixed and reformed to separate us. No one ever spoke to me twice.

No matter what else, I-as-girl never forgot to look back. Each time, I marked the mountains on the far horizon. How the mass melded together save for peaks glittering in the sun. So long as they glowed there, I knew from whence I came and where to head should I escape. I held that hope close when my captor drew my exhausted body around a hillside. A sharp pain made me jerk as he cut my wrist. Hot, dry lips fastened around the wound as he slurped up my blood.

Then I looked to find the mountains gone from sight. Head turning this way and that, I searched all across the horizon. Few signs remained of our passage, save tracks across hard ground—some already beginning to vanish as the wind blew dust and bits of bracken about.

The rising sun beat against my eyes, making my vision blur and tears, precious water, trickle down my face, yet the mountains did not appear. They'd moved or we had, and I was too far to know which way was home. East to the sun, yes, but where else? How could I escape and run home without knowing which way to go?

I sank to my knees, hands trembling. Again and again, I stared at the horizon until my captor yanked me to my feet. I knew better than to fight, now. It won me nothing but hard blows and a gag. Bending my head, I trudged along but kept glancing back in hopes this time I would recognize something.

As a spirit of water, I shivered with my host. Pain and hurt spoke to me, crossing between her and me. In return, I shared a sense of the glade where I belonged. The trees growing near. The flowers blooming along the path of my waters. Birds soaring overhead. Most important: the rocky hillside from whence my waters sprang and the deep power below that was my source.

We'd traveled far, but not left the compass of the deep spirit of the land. As the spring, I knew where I belonged. No matter where my waters flowed upon this earth, I could find the way back.

This I-as-spring shared.

I-as-girl found comfort.

At which, I-me-Mara woke up to a dry mouth and body covered in a layer of sweat even though I'd kicked off my sheet in the night.

What a horrible dream! It didn't take a psychology degree to connect the dots between me leaving home for a longer time than ever before and dreaming about Grampa's tale. That the dreams moved beyond events in his story troubled me, but not for long. I'd overslept and the smell of eggs and pancakes—Mom making my favorite breakfast—got me up and moving.

I turned fumble-fingers soon as I left the bed. Misbuttoned my jeans twice. Almost tied my sneakers together. Dropped scrambled eggs on my blue-and-white Liberty Bell T-shirt so I had to change and leave it behind in the laundry.

Even with those small delays, time came to say good-bye too soon. The sun had barely hatched above the horizon when I went outside. Trying to stifle a sniff, I squeezed Louie close. He brushed a sloppy, open-mouth kiss on my cheek, then protested and wriggled away.

"Have a lovely time. See lots of sights and bring back memories." Mom gave me a warm, firm hug and pat on the back. "We'll miss you, but it's time for you to go off and have an adventure of your own.

"If that's all you want, I can have adventures here." I scuffed my foot against the gray, stone stoop. "Somebody has to take care of Louie, and what if the landlord sells the building like he's threatened and they raise the rent, or—"

She laid a finger across my mouth, then laid a warm arm around my shoulder. "We'll be fine, you know that. Family will pitch in—"

"And preach." A chunk of Mom's family lived on the far side of the city, far enough away we usually got warning before they descended. Not far enough away to keep them from sticking their noses in our business, though, and sniffing because she'd the nerve to have two kids by two different men without marrying either.

"They mean well. And so do I. Maybe this is the same meddling they do, but you're eighteen. You need to go off on your own some. Plus, you didn't get to say good-bye to your father before he died. Maybe spending time with Ignacio will help make things better."

"Grampa isn't Dad." I glanced up and down the street. The usual neighbors were out, passing on their way to or from work and gawking at the loaded road runner. No one unexpected in sight. Hallemay watched as Grampa said bye to Louie, with all of them pretending not to see me and Mom still talking.

"No. He's still alive."

I scuffed my shoe again.

"Your father's dead, Mara." Mom's grip tightened along my back. "You think I don't notice when you check along the street every time you leave the building, just in case he'll come around a corner?"

"I know, I know." Gritting my teeth helped me keep from glancing up and down the block again. "But if anyone could survive, he'd have done it. Remember when the bus hit him and he just bounced up? Or the lamp fried as he was plugging it in, but all he got was first degree burns?"

"The plane crashed. No one survived." Mom hugged me,

tight. "So go spend time with your Grampa. He's the next best thing to your dad."

She had her face tucked into my shoulder so I couldn't see her thinking how my dad wasn't that best to begin with. Not that she ever said as much to my face, but sometimes her voice got loud when she chatted with her sisters about easy-come, easy-go rambling men.

But he was my only Dad, and Grampa made a poor second-best. Still, I nodded and hugged her back until I couldn't put letting go off anymore.

"Call me when you want. Don't mind the charges."

"Grampa said he'd pay, anyway." Nice of him, but it wouldn't be the same. We'd have to condense whole days into a few scrambled, staticky minutes. Louie might get sick or the plumbing bust again and not only wouldn't I be here to help out, I might not even know.

"Call when you need me." She slipped something soft and warm into my hands.

Pulling back, I lifted the lightweight, rectangular object. Stiff pseudo silk covered the edges, deep blue except at the corners where the color had worn away to gray. One side had a solar panel. The other appeared blank until Mom tapped the surface three times. An instant later, a screen came to life offering me the option to call home or dial another number.

It still took moments for me to grasp what I held.

"A satellite phone." Satellites provided the most reliable form of phone connection. With this, I'd always be able to reach her, except maybe out in the middle of a desert. "You shouldn't have. It's too—"

"Hush." She ran a finger across my lips. "It's so you won't worry too much, so I won't have you worrying about the cost either. Besides," she smiled. "I got it second-hand. It's a bit battered around the edges, but works fine."

"I'll call every night."

"If you want to. If you're having fun and skip now and then, I don't mind. Or if things go bad and you need to come home, you say the word and we'll figure it out somehow. Though, I don't think you will. We'll miss you, but I hope you have a beautiful adventure."

Much as I wanted to run back inside the apartment, I slipped into the backseat of the car. It had only two long doors and Grampa couldn't get in until I was settled. Tripods, bags with cameras and lenses, a small travel tote, and other stuff covered half the dark blue seat, leaving just enough room for me. After turning this way and that, I slouched with the seatbelt tight across my hips and shoulder. The buckle dug in, pressing against my jeans. A light pine scent filled the car, stronger on the driver's side. I liked the scent, but it didn't smell of home.

Our travel bags had gotten squeezed into the way back alongside a big old water tank—a weird plastic contraption set within a protective metal cage. Tank and cage were collapsible and took up half the space they would if extended all the way.

The day before, I made the merest suggestion that we leave the water behind or go with a few gallon jugs while in the East because we could always fill up along the way. Grampa turned thunderous, eyebrows lowered and arms crossed over his chest. Where he lived in the Southwest, no one went anywhere without ample water, and no matter how good municipal water systems might be they didn't come close to the water from his home.

That said, Grampa did agree last night to siphon off a couple of gallons and shrink the tank a bit. He filled nearly every empty jug and pitcher in the house, leaving the water for Louie to drink because my brother liked the taste so much. As a result, everything fit in the car—barely.

The water in the tank shook and sloshed as Grampa got in, rocking the car until he'd settled his walking stick along the side. Fortunately for me, he didn't have long legs.

Mom and Louie stood on the stoop waving, but Hallemay delayed us. She'd never quite explained how we were related, other than telling me to consider her a big sister. Grampa was paying her to drive us in her car, but she got to pick the route. Her long-fingered hands gleamed a deep ruddy brown in the sun as she snatched up her camera. The flowing blue fabric of her sundress whirled and her hundreds of waist-long micro braids whistled in the air as she turned in a circle and snuck in a half-dozen photos.

The early morning sun glittered on the raindrops remaining from a brief, early morning shower. The sunshine smudged the street's usual dinginess.

She tucked the camera into a bag near me and slipped into her seat, the water in the tank sloshing. A quick turn of the key made the solar motor whuffle up into a low thrum, and then we were off.

I twisted as much as the seat belt let me, watching Mom and Louie wave until we were out of sight.

ON THE WAY

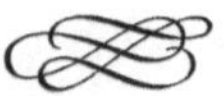

Going away—really away—didn't hit me hard at first. We drove through the city, and things didn't look too different. Row houses lined the streets, with cars and pedicycles parked in front except before flex bus stops.

Parks here, museums there.

More row houses, then stand-alone houses with actual lawns and gardens.

A rose bush danced across a ragged lawn, leaving fallen petals behind. Trees rustled and whispered in the wind, so loud I could hear them, especially since the syngas engine had kicked off and the car glided on the solar motor instead. A big old oak rippled its roots in the moments while we passed. The road twisted beneath us.

We got out of Philly, but not any way I'd have ever guessed—and not on any of the Great Roads.

Those times Mom had the cash, I got to go on school day trips. Twice to New York City and once down to D.C., plus other trips closer by. Each time the bus hopped onto one of the Great Roads. We got all the fun of going fast, keeping on the straightaway, not getting lost—and staying away from shifting lands.

Because the problem with anything being able to move on unfixed lands—plants, trees, boulders, even the land itself—was that the way changed. People got lost a lot.

It wasn't always that way. Plants and trees didn't really start moving much until a generation or two after the Revolution, as though the earth decided to get in on the action, or so one history teacher joked. A couple of students laughed at that, including me.

The movement was mostly in the west at first. Then the joining of the transcontinental railroad somehow sent a wave of unfixing all across the continent—the Railway Quake. Natural accident or terrorist attack or whatever. Independence Hall moved back from the street a meter while City Hall and its foundations did a 180. Many of the tribal nations used the quake and following havoc to wrest back control of wide swathes of land. So did all sorts of other groups. The aftermath left the maps of most states and some cities looking like Swiss cheese: full of holes where different groups had taken over territories.

Mother Earth got a lot more respect.

It took decades for things to shake out, both physically and politically. Some things got fixed back in place, and most towns and cities held together. Philly leaders wound up making a new treaty with representatives of the Lenni-Lenape, who regained control over part of the city. Congress dissolved until the states and added territories revised the Constitution.

All the same, the way to get between fixed places changed whenever land had a whim to move—until President Marshall convinced the Reconstituted Congress to fund the Great Roads. They lengthened or shortened depending on how the land shifted, but guaranteed to deliver you to specific end point exits. One went through Philly North-South with another East-West.

And Hallemay wasn't taking them.

The more I looked around, the more I noticed movement. Maybe some was due to the wind, but not the dancing bushes or the two saplings fighting over a place in the sun. All the shifting creeped me out. I huddled back against the lumpy camera bags, arms wrapped tight across my chest.

Some time later, I don't know how long because I was too busy watching everything move around us, we flashed by a green-and-white sign. A lane to the right led off to a Great Road. We'd got back to some kind of civilization, with more houses and lawns, but Hallemay ignored the turn-off and kept on going, right under the bridges.

"Why aren't we on a Great Road?" Try as I might, I couldn't keep out the whine.

"Feel that?" Hallemay took a deep breath, chest rising and falling, and smiled. "That's freedom out there, to go where you want. Can't find that on the Great Roads. Oh, they'll flex a bit here and there, but the whole purpose is to get you exactly where you think you should go. They make my skin itch."

"Then how are we going to get to Santa Fe?"

"The old-fashioned way: we'll follow a path." She patted the steering wheel.

"But the road can go anywhere." So far, she'd driven mostly on two-lane roads. This meant going more slowly than on the Great Roads, meandering more, and likely getting lost. I'd expected three or four days on the road before arriving at Grampa's home somewhere outside of Santa Fe. No way did I want to spend twice or more time cooped up in the car with him or Hallemay for all I liked them.

"It can. We won't." She shrugged, slowing the car before

turning right onto another two-lane route. The sun rose higher in the sky, heating the metal overhead and warming the car. Rather than turning the air conditioning on, Hallemay cranked the windows down. My hair started to whip around, so I pulled out the tie holding it into a pony tail and braided it.

What had I agreed to? I'd trusted Hallemay not to let Grampa whirl me off on a complete goose-chase.

Then again, I'd never driven anywhere with her before.

"Don't worry, Mara. We'll get where we need to in good time." Grampa twisted in his seat to smile at me even as he raised his voice over the breeze. Then he sat back, tilted his head to the side, and gave Hallemay a quizzical look. "Haven't you told her?"

"Told her what, Grandfather?"

"About your . . ." He gestured at the road ahead of us.

"There didn't seem to be any need before now," she said. "May I?"

She pursed her lips in thought for a while, then nodded.

"Hallemay's a pathwalker," Grampa said.

"But . . . you didn't have any trouble staying with us in the city. Don't pathwalkers hate cities?" Based on times she'd visited Mom and me before, she didn't have any trouble staying in Philly.

"Many can't bear to stay on fixed land very long, that's true enough." She shook her head and made a clicking sound, audible even over the hum of the motor and whistle of the breeze. "I manage, but my real problem is staying in any one place very long. The road keeps calling me, and it's hard to resist. My gift is meant for movement, for choosing which way to go. Take this intersection, for instance . . ."

She stopped the car where two equally small roads met. Houses lined each side, several yards between them with foot-high carved stones marking property boundaries. This house had red trim and that one green. Someone mowed one lawn regularly while another grew weeds jigging in the wind.

They might be different, but down deep they all looked alike to me. Sweat beaded on my forehead and damped the small of my back, making my shirt stick to the rough, cloth seat cover.

"If we turn right, we'd be turning around and retracing our steps within an hour. Now, straight ahead would actually get us to Santa Fe faster, but," Hallemay pointed to the left, "this feels better to me, so that's where we'll go."

Which we did, since she was driving after all. The car rattled away as we headed on. The change of course didn't seem to make any difference until, two turns later, Grampa gave a short bark.

"Ha!" He pointed to a small brown-and-white sign bearing an arrow and a single word.

Zoo.

"Your gift has done it again." He clapped Hallemay on the shoulder. "Let's go see what these alligators have to say."

"I don't mind taking the time. You're the one paying the bills this trip." She shrugged. "Though if you ask me, I'd skip the alligators and head home as straight as we can. Meeting the rest of the family made a difference for me, after all." But she went ahead and followed the direction of the sign.

Apparently, we were going to a zoo. Twice in two days. If only Louie were here, he'd love that. Me? Not quite so much. One every now-and-next-decade would do for me.

Then again, I'd already guessed my role for the summer was to make sure Grampa had a good time. How to make sure of this? Easy enough to answer, harder to do. I'd have to help him find the conquistador, whatever-his-name. Yeah, right, find him in a couple of weeks or months when Grampa'd spent years looking.

And learning how to talk to alligators, which still sort of freaked me out.

"You really think alligators will know where this Torres guy is?"

"Eh?" Grampa twisted around.

I repeated the question.

"They'll know where he isn't, or wasn't when they were captured. Alligators see much more than you imagine, and they have a vested interest in keeping tabs on him." Grampa hrrumphed. "Most don't like him."

"Does anybody?" I meant to be sarcastic, and rolled my eyes, but it came out more serious.

"He can make himself quite agreeable when he wants to."

Something made me swallow my first, smart-aleck response and take a closer look. Grampa's head tilted down, hair swept to one side, and he'd closed his eyes.

"You knew him." Not a question, though others sprang to mind. Where had they met? Had Grampa known who he was?

"Yes. Once upon a time, very long ago."

"Why didn't you just drink from the spring of life when you were with him?"

"What?" The seat back in front of me jerked as Grampa stiffened. His head and hands shook as he turned around very slowly. His mouth gaped open, chest heaved, and dark eyes were open wide.

"Isn't that why you want to find him?" I shrank back against the seat, which squeaked. A sour taste filled my suddenly dry mouth. "To drink and get young again?"

"There is so much wrong in that." He rubbed his forehead with the back of one shaky hand, "Didn't you hear the tale I told yesterday? Torres trapped the spring of life in the body of a young girl. In her blood, which he drank to extend his life long past due reckoning. Not for any cause would I drink the blood and pain of another." Tears edged his eyes, though he blinked them away as he stared at me. "You think that of me?"

"No, no!" I shook my head, a lump in my throat. "I didn't mean . . . I wasn't clear. I mean, I know he put the spring of life in the girl's blood but I thought after all this time . . . maybe there was another way to drink it . . . which you wouldn't, if it was in her, but you never said why you did want to find him."

"Grandfather, you only told her how Torres stole the spring yesterday. Don't rush her." Hallemay took a hand off the wheel long enough to press one of Grampa's hands.

"Truly, I'm sorry. I just didn't think it all through." And how. Stupid, but I'd been treating the whole thing as half-joke as well as half-serious. Yet Grampa meant everything he'd said about the story and the spring.

"Here, have some water, Grandfather. That'll ease you." Hallemay pulled a flask from between the seats. "The family would never forgive me if you had a heart attack on the trip."

Way to make me want to bang my head against the side of the car for being so stupid, and vow to do better. Grampa drained the flask in three long gulps, throat working. His shoulders eased within moments.

"You drink, too." Hallemay passed another flask back to me. "I know where to find most of the best springs in the land, and you won't find better water anywhere."

My fingers curved around the metal, somehow still cool despite having sat in the sun. The water came from the tank in back, I presumed, and tasted as good as yesterday. The faint hint of flowers flushed the tang of bile from my mouth.

"You ask why I want to find him?" Grampa sighed. "For justice, reparation, and vengeance."

"What do you want to do, spit in his eye?"

"That's actually not a bad idea, from a safe distance of course." He gave me a small smile over his shoulder.

"Of course." I sighed, too, settling back into my seat. All might not be forgiven, but he wasn't holding it against me.

"And then I'll kill him."

He'd said it with a straight face, absolutely serious, and yes he seemed in good shape for an older man, but all the same I couldn't visualize it.

"Okay . . . but first we've got to find him."

"True enough." Grampa nodded.

The fresh scent of cut grass filled the car as Hallemay slowed down to make a turn past a man mowing his lawn.

"So, where did you last see him? Should we start there?" I took another swig of water, then held the flask against my face to cool my cheeks.

"The last I saw of him was along the Rio del Norte, near El Paso." Grampa said.

"The what?"

"Rio del Norte, also known as the Rio Bravo or Rio Grande." He waved a hand and shrugged. "But that was long ago. I kept track of him for a while, until I was distracted. The alligators will know."

Having alligators lead us to the conquistador didn't sound like much of a plan to me – but Grampa was more lackadaisical about it than I'd have expected.

As it turned out, though, the alligator at the Maryland Zoo didn't know. The zoo didn't have any American alligators. A Chinese alligator was visible, rather smaller with gray-green scales and a short snout. The head looked cute, resembling the dragon art on Louie's walls at home.

On the other hand, it didn't know anything about Eyague de Torres and wasn't at all happy to have Grampa burbling at it. Even I, who didn't know how to talk to alligators, could tell that much. It made a loud bang, which sounded like a truck backfiring, and stomped away to the far side of the enclosure.

A slender-snouted crocodile nearby, much bigger than the Chinese alligator, echoed the call and doubled the ear-blasting noise.

Grampa stomped away, muttering words under his breath as we wound back through the crowds to meet Hallemay who'd picked up lunch. All told, we were in and out of the zoo in under an hour. A waste of money, as even Grampa admitted.

I didn't mind leaving early one bit, apart from regretting the cost. Passing all the cool animals sunning in their enclosures made me miss Louie something fierce, for he'd have loved it even two days in a row.

So we popped back into the car, fueled up, and headed south again. Understandable at first, because Hallemay skated us down side roads to the Smithsonian Zoo which did have American alligators. They weren't anywhere near as cute as the Chinese, having much bigger and heavier snouts. The larger stretched a good three or more meters and had green mold or something speckling its scales. The smaller, closer to two meters, had darker scales and gave a mighty roar as we approached.

For near twenty minutes, Grampa talked with them. He twisted his sinewy frame in all sorts of directions to produce burbles, rippling trills, and purr-chomps. The movements had a certain grace to them, almost as though he did a sinuous, snaky dance. I tried to copy the shoulder roll and it was harder than it looked. Hallemay hung around taking photos of the alligators and Grampa and me.

Grampa seemed satisfied by the end. The alligators hadn't seen Torres, but they at least knew of him. The last word they'd had, before being brought to the zoo, was that he still hung around near El Paso though he'd been known to travel as far south as Brownsville, Texas, and at least once or twice as far north as Albuquerque.

After which Hallemay drove us off in the same direction, just far enough to get clear of the city and find a small town with a nice, clean motel to stay the night. She and I shared a room, but she told me to take as much time as I wanted to call home. After which she went into the bathroom and water started running in the tub, offering me privacy.

Mom picked up on the first ring.

"Hi Mom."

"Mara." A deep sigh, but before she could say anything more Louie burst out calling to talk to me. She put him on, and we talked alligators for at least five minutes before Mom got the phone back.

"He misses you. We both do, but it sounds as though you're starting well."

"Well enough." I'd had fun. All the same, it didn't hold a patch on taking trips with Dad. He always filled them with special moments. Grampa didn't have that same touch.

"Don't go expecting anything in particular. Let yourself be surprised." Mom must've guessed where my mind headed.

"Yeah. Okay."

"Such enthusiasm. He's not your dad," a sharp breath, then she said, "and you know what my family always says about comparisons."

"They're odious." I'd heard that often enough.

"So give him a chance."

"I am." My turn to go sharp.

"Of course. Enjoy yourself. The summer will fly and be over before you know it."

We said good-byes and hung up. The call left me sitting saggy back on my bed. It wasn't fair to compare traveling with Grampa with Dad, but I did it anyway.

Hallemay emerged from the bathroom and settled on the

other bed. She wrapped a length of blue silk cloth around her head, covering her hair.

"Ready to go sleep?"

"Yeah." I slipped under the thin, cream top sheet.

With a click, she turned off the light. Our room was at the far end of the first floor, Grampa next door. A narrow band of light shone at the bottom of the burgundy curtain across the window. Otherwise we were in darkness. The occasional whizz of a car passing sent faint reverberations through, but otherwise all was still and so very, very quiet.

"How's the first day?" Hallemay asked.

"Okay, I guess." I managed a laugh. "Lots of alligators."

"Yeah." She sighed and shifted in bed, the sheets rustling and mattress creaking.

"You ever learn how to talk to them?"

"No. It takes time, and I don't often stay in one place for long. My road calls me, and it's hard to resist for anything smaller than family. Alligators don't make the cut. You, now, you could learn."

"Maybe." I tried the shoulder roll again, first one and then the other. To my surprise, a small burble escaped me.

"That's the way." Hallemay chuckled. "I'm sure Grandfather'd be most happy to teach you."

"Mm." I grabbed a flask from the table between the beds. The metal sparkled a little as I took a swig of water. Good reason not to answer.

"Ask him. He wants this time with you to go well." More rustling, a creak, and a sigh. "But take the time you need, too. Go at your pace, not his. He's a riddle of an old man. If he tries to rush you, let me know. I'm not above telling him to go walking until he's got his temper back buttoned down. He'll listen to me, because I've been where you are."

"Which is where?"

"Near the beginning of the story, only my beginning was long ago and under very different circumstances."

"If . . . if you don't mind, what were they?"

A long silence, and for a moment I was sure I'd offended her. We'd never spent this much time together before. She tended to pass through once or twice a year, and we'd meet up somewhere for a meal. Or, on longer stops, do something. Visit a museum, or go for a hike in one of the city parks. Now, knowing she was a pathwalker, the element of movement fit.

"You've never asked me that before."

"Mom always told me not to pry. Let people choose what they want to share." My tongue kept going, though maybe I should've shut it. "That way maybe they'd keep their noses out of our business, too."

"That sounds like your mother. Good advice, too, for the most part." Some more rustling of the sheets. "This isn't the time or place, but ask me again when we're in my home—the place I most call home, at least—and I'll tell you more. For now, though, I'll give you something. I first met Grandfather long ago, when I was younger than you if not by much. The War had wrought havoc on land. Fires burned our crops, and we were starving. My mother dying . . ." Her voice broke for a moment. "I tracked my father down, to ask for help. Beg if I had to. Maybe he would have helped, I'll never know. He ran away, because Grandfather showed up. Tracking my father but finding me instead. *He* helped. Lent me money he couldn't easily afford at the time, and aided me in transporting seed and food and medicine back across the lines in time to help my mother live a little longer. At least long enough to know I had other family willing to live up to the name."

I lay in my bed, hardly daring to breathe and scrambling

to think of something to say. I hadn't any notion of what she'd gone through.

"I'm sorry."

She drew in a deep breath and exhaled slowly. "I owe Grandfather." A dry chuckle. "Though not enough to drive you for free. I have my living to earn. And I've paid him back already in the coin he most wanted, though I did it for other reasons. Still, he has always been there for me, and I would do just about anything for him."

If it was meant to soothe me, it failed. This was day one. I had a whole summer to go. Maybe, just maybe, Mom's prediction would come true and it'd end before I knew it. Or not. Curiosity itched me under the skin—which war had Hallemay meant? I'd been sure she was born and raised in the United States and Allied Territories, but we hadn't had a war on this continent for decades. Unless she was even older than I'd thought. But given her approval of Mom's advice not to ask, I'd have to wait to see if she decided to share any more.

I slipped down further under the sheet and lay back. The soft sound of breathing in the next bed shifted, growing louder bit by bit as it edged into a snore—for which, oddly enough, I was quite grateful. Without it, everything verged on silence with few of the regular night noises I was used to. Only one source of tinny music and voices through the walls, not four or five. Occasional whooshes of cars passing along the road rather than longer, rhythmic rumble of flex trains rushing along their regular routes.

As I fell asleep, Hallemay's snoring turned into the roar and crash of waves on land. The horizon stretched out far ahead, filled with long, gray-blue waters rolling towards me. Several ships bobbed out on the water. Dark wood gleamed against the distant blue sky, boasting three or four tall masts each although the sails were furled and little more than white smudges.

Three large rowboats or dinghies or whatever lay beached half out of the water. Men wearing dirty white shirts, brown jackets, and brown pants which ended just below the knee toted barrels, boxes, and cloth-wrapped parcels from piles on land to load into the boats. More finely dressed men in reds and blues, with tall hats, supervised.

Sweat mixed with a heavy brine smell filled my nose, so strong it should have woken me up, but no. I dreamt and knew myself dreaming.

At least, I-me-Mara did. Once again, I found myself lodged within a body that didn't belong to me, sharing space with two spirits, neither of whom acknowledged my presence.

They talked to each other, now—sort of. Ideas and images slipped between them, passing through me in the process, and they had names for each other, or what passed for names. The spirit of the spring was Spring and the feel of sweet-scented waters trickling over earth. For its part, Spring seemed to associate the girl with a full rainbow arcing over mountains familiar from my earlier dream.

Of the two, Spring shrank more away from the sea than Rainbow. It took control over the shared body, twisting and trying to get away from strong hands clamped on our shared shoulders. The rough cloth of the shift covering us scratched our skin.

A whap on our head made our neck crack, immediately soothed and eased as the spring's power went to work.

I couldn't see the man holding us, but Spring and Rainbow knew him. The image of their captor, accompanied by ruddy flares of hate and fear flashed between them. Rainbow took control, bowing her head although my hands ached with the strain of her not closing hers into fists.

"Get in the boat," he said in Spanish. It didn't much

resemble the language I'd spent several years half-learning in school, but the phrase required little translation.

Rainbow clambered over the side, slipping in the layer of smelly water lining the bottom of the boat. She huddled next to a barrel, watching as their captor joined them. Laborers pushed the boat out into the sea, then hopped in and took up the handles of long oars.

A harsh voice called, and the oars dipped nearly as one. The boat lurched, then glided out towards the waiting ships. Water sprayed wide, tasting of salt and brine.

Spring shivered, making the blood within Rainbow surge and her heart beat faster. It held onto the thin thread connecting it to the spot on land where it belonged, no matter how far away. The growing depth of sea between the boat and land—both dry and the sea bed far below—tore the thread and left it loose and flailing.

It shared the image of its home with a sharp, bitter blast of loss. Fear. Horror.

In my earlier dream, Spring had reassured Rainbow they could find their way back following that thread.

Now Rainbow held the spirit trapped within and calmed it. Patience, she shared, be patient. Someday, somehow we'll make it back where we belong.

I woke bolt upright in the bed with my hands clenched tight on the cheap, cotton sheet. My heart pounded hard and my breath came in pants. It took two tries to let go of the sheet so I could press cold fingers against my aching chest.

Forcing myself to lie back, I changed Rainbow's assurance to fit my situation. Someday soon, I'd be back where I belonged. It was just a dream, nothing more than my subconscious using Grampa's story to explore my going far away for the first time and longing for home.

Except, the taste of the sea lingered in my mouth.

SPEAKING WITH BREEZES

*A*nother day, another alligator or, in this case, several.
All in all, we could've skipped this zoo, too, if only Hallemay hadn't made the mistake of mentioning its existence to Grampa at breakfast. She winked at the time, which I took to mean us being in this together in humoring the old man.

Then she dropped me and Grampa at the entrance. Oh, she pleaded errands, but abandoned me to escort him into the reptile house and back. She even had the nerve to wink at me again, same eye and all, before waving and tootling off.

Grampa could've made his own way in and back. He hardly needed me. Didn't wobble at all as we walked to the reptile house. His cane seemed to be an affectation mostly useful for pointing, clearing away trash, and occasionally giving me a poke when I lagged behind yawning because I hadn't got anywhere near enough sleep the night before, what with being in a strange bed and strange town, Halle-may's snores, and the awful dream.

I wore jeans and a plain green T-shirt, and had a jacket on over, but I still shivered in the early morning air. A cool breeze blew around, even though we were inside the reptile house. Someone must've turned the air conditioning up, maybe to try and clear out the odd, musty smell. My toes, bared by my black wrap-around sandals, twitched and rills of chills ran from them all the way up my spine.

We weren't getting much of anything out of it, though this was the fourth time Grampa paid admission fees. I didn't want to think about how much money he was spending even if he had saved up.

Especially because no way could these young, no longer than a meter, alligators be of much help. Zoo-born and zoo-raised, how would they know anything? There were only three of them, or maybe a fourth because the odd-shaped stick at the back had twitched once.

Yet Grampa stood there, burbling and rippling away, without any of them doing much more than flicking a tail now and then.

The breeze kept blowing around us, too, though I couldn't see any air ducts, just the occasional drain in the floor. Cool, cool, and colder, and whistling in my ears. I covered them with my hands, to warm them and block the high-pitched sound, only to have the whistling convert to whispers. Nothing coherent, mind, just wisps. I played around with them in my head, while watching Grampa do his thing, and managed to turn them into an interrogation.

<Have you seen this man?>

An instant later, the image of a man formed before me for a few moments—laid on in mist or smoke redolent of sandalwood. A tall man in a wide-skirted green coat with matching vest and breeches, white lace at neck and wrists, resembling the paintings of the Founding Fathers regularly plastered around Philly, complete with one hand braced on the hilt of a sword hanging from his waist. Dark hair fell to the nape of his neck. A few pocks marred the right side of his rectangular, beige-colored face. Full lips parted in an exultant smile as deep words resounded in my head: la vida eterna.

Then wisps of color flickered in my mind, fitting together as jigsaw pieces to form the sense of an immense, lashing alligator with scales of deep green. An odd vegetative scent overlaid the sandalwood. The sound of rushing water filled my ears, so strong I glanced around to be sure no pipe or cave had broken and started gushing out.

After a few moments, the image of the crocodile grew bigger. Immense jaws opened wide, showing dozens upon dozens of sharp, white teeth. A smaller alligator, top scales almost black and belly scales bright green, materialized as well. Short, stubby legs tried to muscle away, but the big alligator's jaws slammed shut and chopped it in half.

I jerked and jumped back until I had a good, hard surface behind me and nothing could sneak up on me.

A hiss behind me made me whirl around to realize I'd backed against a case holding a bright green snake with a coffin-shaped head. Its glossy skin stood out even amidst the brilliant foliage filling the case.

The snake's dark eyes fixed on me through the glass. My lungs seized and I had trouble catching my breath. I swayed, unable to move, captured by the gaze.

"You can't kill her." A warm arm wrapped around me and Grampa rested his head on my shoulder. An extra burst of heat rippled through my veins. "Don't even try."

Another cool breeze whipped around us, fluttering the tip of my braid. Even the leaves in the cage shook. I jumped at the sensation of fangs latching into my right arm. My left hand rubbed up and down, finding only skin covered in goose bumps and every hair standing on end.

The snake slithered up into the tree branches, although

not without a last flick of its tail. The cold eased. A few shivers rippled through me as my skin returned to normal.

Reptiles and tails. I'd had more flicked at me in the last couple of days than I'd have ever imagined. Easier to think about that, more calming, than how easily the snake had me fixated. Without the glass, I might've stood still for the bite.

"You talk to snakes, too?"

"Not I, but the breezes. They speak for me." He tilted his head to the side and gave a rueful smile. "Sometimes. The weaker the breeze, the more flighty. Literally. I can generally rely on their kindness to translate, but not their retention. Winds, now, if a strong wind promises something, it's as good as done."

"I'll keep that in mind." Over in the alligator pen, four motionless bodies lay prone on the ground. "Did they tell you anything?"

"Nothing of worth. They accused me of telling tall tales of boogeymen and monster alligators who eat those foolish younglings that stray across their paths." Grampa shook his head. "One never knows, and better to stop and ask than not."

Yeah, maybe, but it was his mention of monster alligators that caught me.

"Alligators eat their young, right?" The small ones floating in the man-made river seemed too somnolent, though they could move fast when they wanted to. In water at least, for I'd seen one race from one side of the enclosure to the other lickety-split.

"Sometimes alligators eat each other. The smaller are more likely to be prey, but even larger ones will sometimes be killed and eaten. And these," Grampa nodded at the young and small, "have heard tales of monster alligators who kill and eat all others they meet with. Massive alligator meets small alligator." He joined his hands together at the wrist, palms apart, as though alligator jaws, then snapped them shut. "Crunch. End of tale."

"I saw that." I flinched, because the gesture was so like the image of the big alligator cutting the small in half. What I'd seen matched his tale pretty close.

"What did you see?" He touched my cheek with warm fingers.

He tilted his head to the side and started nodding as I described the vision of the man, then the big alligator, then massive alligator eating the small.

"But I don't talk to alligators, burble or ripple or that weird purr-chomp thing."

"The breezes must have translated for you. I prefer not to rely on them, which is why I learned the ways of alligator speech as best I could. The lighter breezes know everything and nothing, for the air spirits constantly fracture and reform into different arrangements. The steadier tend to repeat things over and over until you want to scream." A gust whipped around us, tangling his hair and blowing dust in his eyes so he blinked.

"The breezes are air spirits?"

"What else?"

"I know callers, or sweet talkers, can communicate with elemental spirits, but I don't have the gift." I'd gone through the whole array of tests for magical gifts in elementary school and again in high school without anything to show for it.

"Neither do I." Grampa straightened his hair and snapped his fingers at the breeze. "Just as well, for that matter. Sweet talkers indeed. Say rather callers are cursed to never be able to ignore those spirits who want to communicate with them, although the reverse is also true, and this drives many of them insane. It's those of us who don't have the gift who are the true sweet talkers. We must lure the spirits into speaking with us. The air spirits are the easiest to reach, for many find us fascinating. Perhaps you've become a person of interest to one."

"Huh."

"You doubt me?" He tilted his head to the side, leaning on his cane for once. "Try to converse. Use your breath, even when you do not speak aloud, to share what you want the breezes to know. Keep aware for stray words, images, smells, and senses. The air spirits rarely speak in words alone."

Then how did they speak? I shrugged and turned back towards the alligators, ignoring Grampa's low chuckle behind me.

A cool rill of air ran along my bare arms, making me shiver. Had to be the air conditioning, and yet . . . Grampa's words echoed in my ears, soft and mixed around.

Interest. Sweet talkers. Fascinating. Lure. True. Stray.

If an air spirit had taken an interest in me, sharing words and images, how was I supposed to communicate with it? Grampa didn't look to be of any help on that front. He sat on a bench, head tilted back and swinging his cane around and around. His lips twitched, quirking to the side in a smirk. Just call him a man of mystery and be done. I should be done playing his games, yet I kept getting sucked in.

What if I could talk to breezes? How cool would that be? Something special.

Grampa talked to them. An image formed in my head of him standing, lecturing and twirling his cane, while silvery breezes and gusts of winds whirled about him. It tickled my funny bone. Maybe the breezes would enjoy it too. I sort of pushed it to the edge of my mind, projected it into the air, to see what would happen.

Nothing at first.

Then I exhaled, only a sigh, and the air swirled before me, kicking up bits of dust and bracken. The very scene I'd imagined formed in dust for a moment, then sailed over the barrier into the alligator pond. The sole alligator laying out on land yawned, then snapped at the dust cloud.

A breeze whipped back around, raising waves across the water in its passing.

Cold, wet scales brushed along my arm, and every hair stood on end. Sharp teeth pressed against my skin for a moment. I couldn't see them, but as I ran my hand over my forearm I had to stop half-way as my fingers touched something hard and invisible.

Maybe talking to breezes wasn't such a good idea after all.

RAINBOW

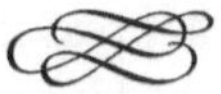

*B*ack in the car, I tried to sleep as we headed on south and west. Easier said than done, because while off running errands Hallemay had shifted bags and packages around. Now a rectangular box sat on the seat next to me. A foot-and-a-half high, it had hard sides and no give whatsoever. Heavier than lead, too, for it squashed the upholstery and made wrinkles at the corners. Try as I might, I couldn't shove it anywhere to get even as much as an inch more to curl up in.

All the same, I managed to fall asleep or at least doze for a bit, only to wake to the car rocking back and forth.

Hallemay tried to squeeze into the backseat next to me an oblong mess of green cloth bound around and around with coarse rope over something solid. The heavy box had vanished, leaving an ebbing dent behind. In its place, she kept trying to angle the big mass through the gap between the car door and driver's seat.

It didn't fit. Even with the driver's seat pushed forward as far as it could go, it wasn't ever going to squeeze in.

"Careful, careful now." A strange woman, wearing

nothing but blue overalls, with thin, waist-long braids cascading around, watched the operation with an anxious expression. A gray farmhouse loomed to one side with a red barn to the other, and the air was redolent with the smell of wet earth.

"This won't work." Hallemay pulled back and laid the package on the ground, then wiped her forehead with her arm. "We'll have to do it the other way round. Sorry, Grandfather, but you'll have to take the backseat for a stretch."

"Of course, this is what happens when you take live passengers. I knew the risks." Grampa nodded. Retrieving his cane from next to the seat, he crossed in front of the car and wound up with one hand on the driver's side door. "Though, I'd be happy to drive—"

"No."

Even Mom never managed that kind of finality.

"You need help or something?" I couldn't resist a jaw-cracking yawn.

"Sorry we woke you." Hallemay smiled at me as she started turfing out the packages and bags from the floor behind her seat, passing them to the stranger. "This is just a changeover and won't take long."

Sure enough, Grampa slipped into the backseat next to me as Hallemay and the stranger stuffed the smaller packages into the kneewell of the passenger seat. They both put the big package on the seat, with the stranger carefully fastening the seatbelt over it.

A few more seconds, then Hallemay got in. She gave the other woman a wave, got one back, and off we went.

"What's this?" I peered around the seat back at the mass of cloth and rope.

"It's my other job, what pays the bills when folks don't want to buy my photos." The car jolted as Hallemay navigated a long dirt road with plenty of potholes. She kept touching the big package with her fingertips, making sure the seatbelt kept it in place.

"Other job?" I blinked. Last time she passed through Philly, she'd taken me down to a gallery showing her work—photos of mountains and rivers and people, most black-and-white but some in color. Given the prices listed for the photos, surely she made a good living that way.

Guess not. Maybe she'd needed a second job once upon a time or perhaps she still did.

"If you care more how something gets from here to there than when, or if who transports it matters, then I'm your person. Well, one of them. There are others, though we don't meet often, except when our roads run together." She sighed. "Otherwise, we're too busy going our own routes."

"So, what're you carrying this time?" Given all the care in packaging, and the odd shape, it could be a piece of sculpture or something arty.

Hallemay shook her head.

"What, don't you know?"

"I know enough to take whatever care's needed, but otherwise it's not any of my business." Swiveling her head around long enough to shoot me a glance, eyebrows raised, she added, "and certainly none of yours."

"Hallemay's very popular." Grampa leaned forward to slide his cane down behind the front seats. The wood scraped against my ankles a couple times until he got it set to his satisfaction.

"I do well enough. There are some folk who'd rather wait until their need calls my road to them than risk sending their treasures on any government or corporate shipping service." Hallemay patted the steering wheel. "It's one way to keep on the road."

"This is cool. I had no idea." The postal service was all I'd ever used, receiving the occasional postcards from Dad, then Grampa, or sending ones to them.

"Well, unless you need a courier such as me, you're not likely to meet us save by chance. I told Grandfather I'd take the two of you cross-country, but the long way round. You're not my only load. I've stops in North Carolina and Georgia before we head farther west. And if my road calls me to another stop, we'll go."

"Who takes us and how we get there matters more than when." Grampa leaned forward to squeeze Hallemay's shoulder. "Though I still think you could let me drive now and then."

She laughed and gripped his hand with hers for a moment, but shook her head. "Not ever happening, old man."

I tried to get back to sleep, but having Grampa next to me wasn't any more comfy than the immovable boxes. They, at least, didn't radiate heat as he did, nor did come with the smell of eggs and onions as Grampa gave the occasional burp.

Plus, he kept moving, either twisting his legs this way and that or tapping his foot or stretching shoulders so they crackled. Every now and then, he knocked the edge of the passenger side front seat, which made whatever was in the box rattle. When that happened, a savory scent filled my nose for a moment or two before dissipating. It seemed familiar, as though I should recognize it but didn't, which irritated me almost as much as Grampa not being still.

Wrapping my arms across my chest, I tried to settle against the side of the car and let the movement lull me back asleep. I might've grumbled a time or two when Grampa moved again.

Or ten.

At which point Grampa turned to me, lips tight.

"What's got under your saddle?"

"Tired. Didn't sleep well last night and can't rest now." Because he kept distracting me.

"Have some water." He grabbed one of the many flasks and bottles kept filled with water from the tank and pushed it on me. "It'll do you good."

"Will it make me grow?"

"Ah, no." He shook his head, mouth twisting. "Time will take care of that."

"Hasn't yet." The cool liquid eased my throat and the ache in my head, though I was still tired as all get out.

"I didn't finish the tale of the spring of life, did I?" Grampa shifted in place again, turning to face me.

"No. You didn't ever really answer how you know it, either."

A snort from the front seat, though Hallemay didn't say anything.

"Well, that's part of the tale, and we'll get there in good time."

"Okay." I might as well bite, as he obviously wanted me to ask. We still had days stuck in the car. "So, what happened next?"

"Let's see, now where did we leave off?"

"The bad guy had carried off the spring of life." I slunk as low as the seatbelt allowed, hoping he wouldn't drag things out much more.

"Ah, yes." He nodded. "Yet even as Torres stole the spring, Coronado retreated back to New Spain with Torres and his captives following in the train. The spring and girl both tried to escape many times, but Torres kept close watch and foiled every attempt."

Grampa shifted and gave a sigh as he settled with his back against the far side of the car.

"But there were those who kept watch on him, too. By the time Torres reached Mexico City, rumors began to rise of the kind no wise man of the time would wish, nor even those not so wise. The kinds of whispers that raised suspicions among the Inquisition. The more youth and vitality flowing in Torres's veins from regular drafts of blood and the spring's water, the greater risk the Inquisition would take him up for questioning. At the first opportunity, he sailed for Spain and carried with him the spring and Rainbow—"

"Wait, Rainbow?" A chill rippled through my body, multiplied by vibrations as the car rumbled over uneven road. Shades of my dreams about the spring and girl learning to speak to each other . . . and the girl being called Rainbow.

"The girl Torres stole. She had many names over the years, most given to her by Torres. India. Barbara." He wrinkled his nose and muttered something I didn't understand under his breath. "Maria, after she was baptized. Melita once. Manuel or Miguel, on those occasions when he had her pretend to be a boy, his page or illegitimate son."

"Then why did you call her Rainbow?"

"That was how the spring addressed her. Remember," he leaned forward, "spirits do not communicate in words alone, but through sights, sounds, smells and more. When the spring and girl . . . existed in the same body, they had no word for 'you,' so they needed something to represent each other. For the spring, it was the sense of water flowing over earth. For the girl, a human and a rainbow."

The sudden sensation of a thousand drops of water rippled over me only to dissolve an instant later. Warmth followed, along with a flash of light bathing me in a full range of colors. Not quite what Grampa had described, but close. Too close.

None of the magical gifts I'd learned about included sensory flashes. Or maybe they did, but only people who had them and got training ever learned about it—which wasn't me.

Grampa watched me, eyes intent and lips twisting to the side.

"Are you all right?"

"How do you know their names?" He had no call to smirk at me.

"We'll get to that later." With an immense sigh, he shook his head and drummed his fingers against his leg. "Much later. When the story reaches that part."

"No, now. If this means so much . . . how the hell would you know what they called each other?"

"You have to hear the story in order." He stopped drumming and gripped his leg instead, fingers digging deep enough the fabric creased and his knuckles whitened.

"But you're not telling it in order."

"I will tell you everything, in the proper time—"

"You can't just go dropping bits and pieces and being all mysterious telling me to wait." I crossed my arms over my chest, holding my own shoulders. The seat belt strap dug into my neck, because I'd backed up to lean against my side of the car.

"They raised him." Hallemay said over her shoulder, then made a swooping turn that rocked both of us.

"Hallemay!" Grampa stretched out a hand to grab her arm, then clearly thought better of it and grabbed the seat back instead.

"I know what you're doing, Grandfather." She took a hand off the wheel long enough to pat his. "But you have to give her something more."

He leaned his forehead against the dark blue fabric covering the driver's seat.

"Who raised you?"

"Torres and Rainbow, though not by those names. They went by Hector and Melita de Leon in those days." He didn't move, voice thin and muffled. "And the Spring raised me too, for that matter, I suppose, though I didn't know it ran in Rainbow's veins. I had no notion. Though, for that matter, I believed them married and myself Torres's legitimate son, neither of which were true. I knew Torres was an alchemist and sorcerer who collected magical antiquities—and that he hit her when he was angered, but not that he drank her blood until long after I left home or maybe I could have . . . I learned the truth when I received a letter from Rainbow laying out her secrets, before she escaped for the last time."

His words resounded in my head at first as empty syllables, only slowly gaining meaning and all kinds of sub-meanings. This was the kind of news that would take minutes, hours, days even to work through. Possibilities whirled through me, but I focused on three core takeaways:

First, Torres was a real person. Grampa wasn't chasing a legend but the man who raised him. His father, whether or not legitimate, which made him my great-grandfather.

Maybe his tale of the theft of the spring of life had more validity than I'd given it credit for so far.

In which chase, Rainbow escaped. Or had she?

"Did she make it?" I asked first.

"He caught her again." Grampa's back heaved.

"What happened then?"

"He lives, she lives."

"And?"

"I promise you'll know the whole story before we get to Santa Fe, but in the proper order."

"Not again." I did, sort of, understand why order mattered to him. I'd jumped over the big surprise about who'd raised him to focus on Rainbow's escape, because the raising would take longer to work through. Still, he could at least tell me how things had ended. Dad never did this. He might not tell me the end at the start, but he always let me know early whether a story had a happy ending or was a tragedy.

"It's not to tease you."

"Tell her why." Hallemay sighed and patted Grampa's hand again. "It'll make a difference."

"Long ago, I told your father the story, but too fast. All in one gulp." Grampa's back heaved again. He leaned back, tilting his head towards the roof of the car. Tears glittered on his cheeks. "Those I've told the story to slowly still speak to me. Hallemay. Her siblings. My other children. But your father spent the rest of his life running away from me. My own son, my firstborn, afraid of me."

Served me right for pushing instead of just letting Grampa tell the tale his way, because sharp pains spiked through my head. Not for long, but I didn't handle pain well, likely because I got sick or hurt so seldom that even the smallest pangs ripped through me.

Too much information!

Worse, nothing fit square. As though someone had mixed up jigsaw pieces from different puzzles and handed me an assortment.

Grampa always chose his words with care when he talked about my dad.

But afraid? My father? That fell so far off the table of all I remembered.

Dad would run into traffic to save a child from being hit by a bus and get whacked himself in the process, no matter he walked away with little more than a limp.

He'd made a career of taking dangerous assignments to report on doings in far parts of the globe where armies surged and seethed.

On the other hand, Dad hadn't ever told me about his family, not even his father. I'd asked years back, about a year before he died, after turning in a family tree assignment which had lots of information about my mother's side but only him on the other, and never learned any more until the day Grampa and Hallemay showed up at the door. I'd only met two other cousins since then, both of whom watched their words when the subject turned to Dad, and loved Grampa to bits.

Which point I hadn't reached, but maybe I sorta, kinda loved Grampa though not the same as Dad. To the point seeing him cry made me want to give him a hug and tell him everything would be okay, even if that was an outright lie because Dad *was* dead and Grampa would never have a chance to make things right between them.

Grampa turned, tears still trickling out of his eyes. He unbuckled his seat belt, which clattered as it hit something on the floor. Leaning forward, he lifted a trembling hand to stroke my cheek.

"Let me tell you slow, so you can take it in by degrees. There's too much at stake." He cupped my head between warm hands. "The last thing I want is to make you run from me, too."

CATAWBA

We stopped for dinner at roadside stand with a long name: *Dinner for a World Turned Upside Down*. The rickety building held only enough space for a few cooks and counter help, plus a window for drive-thru orders. Must've been brutal hot inside, with the sun beating down on the tin roof. Overhangs sheltered picnic tables set close enough to hear birds calling in the trees—and the crackle of peppers and onions frying in the kitchen.

Hallemay discovered people she knew waiting in line—two middle-aged white men, both also pathwalkers. She introduced them as Ian and Sven, and Grampa insisted on their joining us for dinner. His treat.

He sent me over to stand in line and place the order, cash in hand, while he staked out a long, weathered table in full shade, sitting with his back against it and his legs and cane stretched out, patently taking a nap. Hallemay and the other pathwalkers took the end to talk shop, their voices low as they exchanged news.

I studied the walls as I waited in line. Bright yellow paint clung to most of the boards, apart from a few spots of crackling and flaking by the downspout. On their own, they weren't worthy of a second look—but they boasted dozens of small figures mounted along the sides. At least half were humans in all shapes and colors, wearing all manner of clothes. The artist had included a variety of animals, from cats to bison, but they didn't draw the eye much because they appeared right-side up while the humans, one and all, were shown feet up and heads down.

Art imitating life or life art? The ground didn't feel any too solid beneath my feet and this time I knew it was all in my head. Everyone else walked with ease, and the building walls trembled not a whit.

Only one person swayed with each step: me.

No reason for it, and yet it felt true. Too many mysteries in the air, too many unanswered questions. Worse, Grampa had reasons for not being forthright, understandable but damnable reasons.

Given a choice, I'd go back in time and skip starting the unfinished story, but I didn't have the option.

After placing our order, my wayward, tilting feet brought me to the table opposite Grampa. I sat down, propping my heavy head on my hands. The boards beneath my elbows bore witness to the restaurant's popularity—at least as a place to carve images and initials into the wood. KA was here. PH+TO in a heart. Plus cats, deer, horses, and an immense octopus.

Grampa swiveled around, tucking his feet under with ease but hitting the table legs with his cane a couple of times. The bangs reached my ears in time with the vibrations through the wood.

"Are you all right?"

"It's been a long day." He sighed and turned to the side. His hair gleamed, as always, but instead of a solid thatch of snow, the strands thinned here and there to show glimpses of red-brown. "I don't travel much anymore, and I'm starting to remember why."

"You should be home."

I traced the lines of the octopus's arms with a finger, nearly catching a splinter before I slowed to take more care.

"This is the last trip. If I do not finish, others will have to take up the yoke."

"To find . . . Torres?"

He tilted his head to the side in thought for a moment, then shrugged and shook his head.

"To do everything left undone."

Typical. I kept my mouth shut, unable to come up with any kind of decent response. I should've tried something, though, because he didn't say anything either, which meant the silence grew. Oh, pots clattered in the distance, oil spat, and orders were placed. Plus the low hum of cars passing on the main road not far away.

But between us, the silence turned heavy. Thick. Waiting for someone to break and shatter it.

Grampa caved first.

"If you have questions, ask. I promise to answer them, every single one—but in my time, not yours."

If I had . . . I had dozens, except they seemed to be so many marbles set on a counter waiting for the first to break and roll. Until one did.

"I don't get why Dad was afraid and ran from you."

"Ah, yes. Dive in with a hard question." He squeezed his eyes closed tight, wrinkles deepening, then opened his brown eyes and stared directly into mine. "I asked him to do something and he refused. I prefer to believe he was ashamed of saying no, of always saying no, and that was why he avoided me."

"But you don't think that's it."

"I want to believe it, but I will never know. We had a hard

relationship even when he was young. I took many trips then, leaving him with his mother, and he resented it." Grampa sighed, shoulders slumping. "You may run from me too, though not, I hope, so long and hard."

"I won't." This time I grabbed his hands. The notion of my dad being ashamed made me shift as though a dozen fleas took a simultaneous bite. That didn't seem right, not the dad I knew. Yet I couldn't push it, because talking about him hurt Grampa. So I tried to redirect instead. "Especially when you haven't finished the story."

He smiled.

Our order number came up, so I jumped up to get our food. Ian and Sven helped carry it over while Hallemay went back to the car for mugs of the water we'd brought. We wound up with a heaping platter of grilled vegetables, a stack of steaming tortillas, and a quartet of sauces which we placed in the center of the table. To one side lay a smaller platter of crispy plantains dotted with brown sugar butter for dessert.

The conversation turned general as we all pitched into the food. Ian and Sven were headed northwest, on a run carrying packages to points around the Great Lakes.

"And where are you headed?" Ian asked.

"Roundabout." Hallemay filled a tortilla with onions, peppers, and mushrooms. "Catawba, the Carolinas, Georgia, and then likely points west."

"Catawba?" Ian nodded and Sven drew in a whistling breath. "Any word about a certain decision?"

"It might have been made, though I haven't heard anything for certain yet." Hallemay shook her head and touched her lips with a finger. "But better not to dwell on it now."

"Of course."

That was the only part I didn't understand. Otherwise, both men made for good company as they and Hallemay and

Grampa all talked about places they'd been, and engaged in a mock-competition of recommending places I should visit someday—on this continent and others. I didn't talk much, but I ate. Especially the plantains.

I wound up back in the car in a bit of a sugar haze as Hallemay drove southwest and the sun headed down towards the horizon.

At which point, Grampa continued his story.

"Torres left New Spain for Europe one step ahead of the Inquisition, as it were. He remained one step ahead in Spain, but barely." His neck cracked as he turned his head to give me a narrow glance. "I don't know how much your teachers taught you about the Inquisition in school?"

"Some. Not much but some." I'd probably learned more from the occasional documentary or mockumentary on television. "They were organized to root out heretics, right?"

Yes, first through forcible conversion or expulsion of Jews and Muslims, then Protestants and others who might threaten the purity of the Catholic faith.

I cannot argue with the Inquisition's interest in Torres, but no one ever quite caught up with him. All the same, he did not linger anywhere for very long.

He lived to a very specific pattern: move to a new town or city—he tended to vary regions and size—and establish himself as a doctor at first and then, as he grew in wealth through means best not examined too closely, a man of leisure considering buying property in the neighborhood. He could usually manage this for a few years—two, five, ten—before rumors and the occasional traveler recognizing him raised suspicions high enough he had to move away.

When he did move, he traveled light. Never kept servants for long, unless he had something to hold over their heads and ensure both compliance and silence. He didn't trust bribes, or at least only in conjunction with blackmail.

Once set, this pattern remained in place, so far as I am aware. It's what I remember from my youth—move every five to seven years, though by then he wandered at will across Europe. He did so not solely to avoid suspicion of lack of aging, but also in search of magical artifacts—swords, goblets, books, and more—of which he amassed a great many over the centuries.

But I digress. It is the time long before my birth of which we speak. In those first decades, he did have one very close call with the Spanish Inquisition.

At that time, he kept to Spain. Indeed, his very first residence was Seville, where he set up as a physician. He never shared the secret of Rainbow's blood, and didn't give anyone a hint she was magic. The servant he hired to run his house assumed she was his illegitimate daughter.

For he did demand from the servants a certain degree of care for her. Her own bed. Clothes made for her, rather than hand-me-downs, although of plain, hardy fabrics.

And, on her side, a forcible education in what he valued. She was taught to sew, to make and mend her clothes and his. To shop in markets. To cook, or at least oversee the process of cooking and ensure the results were to his taste, along with many other daily tasks—in short, eventually to become his most perfect servant and aide.

My hands lay loose in my lap, yet all of a sudden my fingers twitched as though I held a needle and pushed it through a thick, nubby fabric.

Then, although my hands hadn't moved, they seemed to cradle a smooth porcelain bowl of some kind. My arms ached from the strain of holding it, and my nose wrinkled at the acrid stench of urine. My body jerked as the phantom sensations had me tipping the bowl and then my ears rang as the liquid cascaded down to beat on stones and someone yelled at me in Spanish. I didn't recognize all of the words, but the meaning came through. Barbarian was the kindest of the terms.

I licked my dry lips and found a light sugar residue from dessert. The sweet banana taste flowed through me, banishing the other sensations although not the memory of them.

Grampa didn't seem to notice, though he'd paused to massage his forehead. Noting my gaze, he continued.

All this, but Torres also ensured she converted to Catholicism. You see, he considered himself properly religious. Even when he raised me, it was as a Catholic with church attendance, daily devotions, confession, respect for fasts and saint days and . . . he did not ever consider himself to have turned his back on the Church, although he knew some, whom he considered unenlightened, would argue the point.

Rainbow followed the forms when I was a child, and I thought her a good Catholic then. Only later did she admit she prayed mostly by rote, and sought to keep alive memories of her family and their practices.

But that was later. In the early years, a servant regularly escorted her to a nearby convent. The nuns were kind, she said, at least most. She remembered in particular one who explained the value of reading as a skill, though she did not learn to read until well after they left Seville.

Again the weight of a heavy object pressed on my hands. Soft, tooled leather met my fingers. Brilliant colors obscured the back of the car seat. Instead, intricately decorated bands of red, blue, and green formed two arches over lists of words. One arch held a bull's head within and the other a bird of some sort. A warm hand gripped my shoulder. A woman whispered words I didn't understand, but sounded like Latin.

I shook my head, and the sensations dissolved. I was back in the car, with Grampa's low, crackly voice in my ears.

Most of the priests she met were likewise kind, in particular the one who baptized her, but another scared the nuns and, by exten-sion, her. As it happened, he was an inquisitor.

By this time, Rainbow and Spring had learnt enough of Spanish and the ways of life in Spain to understand something of the danger of the Inquisition, but they did not know enough.

They thought to use the Inquisition to take Torres away. Kill him, by preference, but at the least delay him so that they might find their way back across the sea.

So they dropped hints to the nuns and priests about Torres's collections of books and artifacts, bottles of dust and poison. His experiments with blood.

Alas, in betraying him to the Inquisition, they said too much. Although the nuns protested, the inquisitor took them for ques-tioning.

"By them you mean Torres and Rainbow and Spring?" I asked.

"No, just Rainbow and Spring. Torres escaped before he could be taken." Grampa shook his head, jaw tight. He rubbed his fingers together, making a soft whispering sound. "Although he did not trust bribes alone, he took care to have coin-friends in all important offices and so received advance warning."

Pain tore through me. My fingers and toes curled as my nails seemed gone leaving only bloody welts. A thousand or more pins seemed embedded in the fleshy parts of my palms and the soles of my feet. Warm, unyielding metal pinioned my wrists and ankles. My back arched back at an extreme angle, stretched over a hard, rough surface.

Dinner turned sour in my stomach and I tried to retch, but nothing came from my dry mouth save gasps and moans.

"Torres did not leave, however." I couldn't see Grampa, but his voice rang in my ears. "He came back and freed Rainbow and Spring."

A familiar face appeared before me—the man from my

nightmares. My captor. Hatred flooded through me—I detested no one and nothing in the world so much as him—yet in that moment he was welcome, the more so as the pains began to subside. With clanks and groans, the metal holding my wrists and ankles parted. He threw me over his shoulder and marched away as everything melded into groans, sobs, and gray stones stained with blood and soot.

Returning slowly to my rightful time and place, I cringed back against the soft upholstered seat. Clasped my hands tight, carefully inspecting my fingers and finding no damage, not even scratches. I resisted doing the same for my feet, but with difficulty.

I was safe. Each shuddering breath made the car around me, Grampa beside, and Hallemay up front, both solid and real. More real every moment, their mere presence making me feel a little safer and the horrid hallucinations more distant.

But not gone.

"Torres took them with him to Grenada first. Then Toledo, Valencia, and other cities before he decided Spain was too dangerous. At which point they left for the Netherlands, which the Spanish then ruled."

Grampa stopped there, and just as well.

I didn't protest, not one whit, because my body ached in sympathy from vicarious torture.

Maybe Grampa did have good reason to tell the story slowly, if everyone who listened did more than hear words. If we all received flashes of visions, strange emotion, and physical sensations.

Maybe when he told Dad fast, Dad couldn't deal with the onslaught. So he fled. Except that didn't fit with my memories of him. Oh, he had restless feet for sure. He'd blow in one day to swoop me up and around in a big hug, only to do the same in reverse less than a week later as he left. When he called to check on me, if I mentioned something big coming up, such as the youth choir singing at a church service, he wouldn't promise to make it. All the same, nine out of ten times—okay, say five out of six, he'd be there. And when he did visit, he was up for anything I suggested no matter how short notice.

He could deal with change and strangeness. Indeed, he thrived on it, preferring the new to the mundane. Making everything fun while he was around, then vanishing.

I'd considered myself a mix of Mom and Dad, loving fleeting pleasures but able to survive and thrive in the everyday grind.

At first I'd taken the whole thing as a story. Yes, magic existed in the world, no one doubted that, but nothing I knew about magic quite explained a spring of life. Easy enough to accept springs having spirits, for everyone knew about earth and air spirits. All the same, a spring having the power to heal? Nobody had that, that I'd ever heard. It should be only a story.

Yet the story filled my dreams and sank into my bones, making me live a shadow version.

A hard tap on my forehead pulled me back into reality. I whipped around to glare at Grampa and the self-satisfied smile stretching his face.

"What was that for?" Rubbing the spot made the sting linger, so I yanked my hand away and sat on it.

"So much thought going on in there, all those gears turning." He shook his head. "Sometimes, my dear, thoughts get in the way."

"I thought you wanted me to think things through to the bitter end."

"Yes, but then, at the end, either act or let go." He leaned back and shrugged a shoulder. "What thoughts were turning your mind so far and fast?"

"Just—how real the story is." I stretched, muscles crackling along my back and arms. All the phantom pains had passed. "I could practically feel myself being tortured."

"Of course." He nodded. "It's in your blood."

Before I could react, the car stopped in the middle of nowhere. The road ran on ahead, through thick stands of trees, before winding off into the distance. The heavy wealth of green leaves hid all but the nearest underbrush from sight, but hills and maybe mountains lay to either side given how much the road had bent and curved up and down in the last hour or so.

Hallemay eased off onto the dirt shoulder and put the engine into rest mode with a click. Opening the door, she stepped out and stretched, bending this way and that and emitting at least twice as many cracks as I had. Leaving the door open, she leaned back against the car frame.

Only nature broke the silence at first, with winds brushing through the leafy trees and birds calling in the distance.

"What's wrong?" I was behind the over-full passenger seat, so I couldn't get out. "Did the car die?"

"No." Hallemay smiled over her shoulder at me. "We're waiting."

"For what?"

"For the road into Catawba."

"We're there?" Grampa peered around and shook his head. "I only visited once, but this doesn't look familiar at all."

"You must've gone in by the front way, Grandfather." She tilted her head back and to the side, as though listening to something else. "It's four hours farther along, and that's in good driving light. This is a back way."

A back way to what? I didn't see any signs of civilization and people around, except the road.

"Who, what, where are we?"

"This is the edge of the Catawba nation."

"I thought they were further south in the Carolinas." When I was in school, most students agreed geography was the worst class bar none—because the maps kept changing. Even in Philly, places sometimes moved. The Lenni-Lenape claimed the parklands, for one, and every season they changed which the general public could enter. All the same, I'd seen the main map of North America often enough to know that while Indigenous nations flourished everywhere, most sat west of the Mississippi.

"Not by far. I've heard tell their numbers fell so low South Carolina didn't remove them west on the Trail of Tears, but they never died away. When the world changed, they took their chance. Their governing council reclaimed a large swathe of their original territory, and they keep the land turned just sideways enough to make it hard for outsiders to enter anywhere except a few places, which are carefully monitored." Hallemay stretched again, then folded herself back into the car. "I grew up near a Catawba village and learned some of their language then, and I've made an effort to keep up relationships. I used to drive farther to the front way in, but a year or so ago the council decided to trust me with an introduction to this way."

A big, battered blue truck flying the North Carolina state flag zoomed down the road behind us. The driver honked in passing, loud enough bellows that a pair of jays in one tree swooped out to follow it with mocking caws.

An instant after the truck turned a corner and went out of sight, the trees shifted. Vibrations rocked the car, making my bones jingle and my teeth knock together. Chills ran down my spine as the earth moved to reveal a narrow dirt road leading off into the hills.

The car lurched and jerked as we drove down the bumpy

surface. Another set of vibrations and when I turned to look behind, the trees had moved back to hide the other road. This wasn't much more than a track, barely wider than the car. Overhead, tree branches filled the narrow expanse so that, at least in summer, no one flying above could find the road. Ahead lay the dim recesses of a winding road.

To either side, the trees seemed to watch us. Chestnuts and oaks and maples, moved their branches, rustling as they shifted close enough to brush their leaves against the car windows. The graying light of dusk made everything spooky and strange.

"The Catawba allow you in the back way, but what about me and Grampa?" One maple pressed its leaves hard against the glass separating it from me. "I'm English and French and Scot on Mom's side, and Spanish on Dad's. And they all did some pretty awful things, according to my history teachers."

"Spanish? Is that what Carlos told you?" Grampa leaned his head on his hands. "Oh, my boy."

"Isn't he? I mean, wasn't he?" True, Dad hadn't ever actually said as much. Not that we talked about it on his visits, because there were always so many things to do. Nor was he around the time my fourth grade teacher had us doing genealogical charts. I'd put down Spain because . . . "Dad always said he came from Spain."

"He should have said from Switzerland, the Netherlands, Cochiti, and Spain."

"At any rate," Hallemay broke in, "I've always found visitors are welcome here—though most come through the front doors—so long as they abide by laws of hospitality." She gave a sharp nod. "Trust only goes so far. There are scouts watching, I'm sure. I expect we'll see one soon."

A breeze squeezing through the crack at the top of the window gave me a glimpse of two or three people, no older than me, sitting in a treehouse of some kind. The next moment, a second vision overlaid the first, of a young man in a red-and-white plaid shirt and jeans, with hair as dark and long as mine, riding a gray horse.

The sound of hooves resounded down the road. The trees pulled back their leaves from pressing against the sides of the cars, and a moment later a rider appeared out of the shadows.

He matched the image the breezes had blown my way, down to the smile on his lips which thinned as he saw the car held more than Hallemay.

She pulled to the side and stopped. When he rode close enough, she cranked the window down and said something to him. I didn't understand the words, but vague memories of language group lessons in school helped me identify it as related to Dakota. He replied, smile returning for her, but within moments cantered off back along the track.

Moving the car back onto the track, Hallemay forged ahead. The road got less twisty the farther we drove. Amidst the dark of nightfall, lights appeared in the distance.

"We're expected," she said. "We'll stay here for the night."

VESUVIUS

$\mathcal{A}$ light breeze made the curtains at the window flutter against each other, raising soft whispers as cool air slipped through the gap at the bottom and blew through the room. The chilliest air sank to the floor where I lay on a pallet. Fortunately, the angle of the sun through the windows resulted in thin rays falling across my legs and feet, keeping them warm, but I pulled the soft wool blanket up over my head. The breeze snuck tendrils in under the cloth anyway. My nice new nightie offered little protection, nothing more than a layer of stamp cotton in blue-and-pink checks.

"Leave me be." I rolled onto my side and inched further down, so the sunlight fell as high as my belly. Even under the wool, my shoulders chilled. Then my torso and legs too, as the sunlight dissolved. The breeze would not leave me alone. The blanket kept it out where it lay across me, a welcome weight, but it wasn't tucked in except at the foot of the pallet so the breeze found plenty of gaps to sneak up through. Which it did, bringing gifts.

First it slipped a view of last night's sky across my closed eyes—I saw it nevertheless, and got as awestruck as by the real thing, for I'd never imagined seeing so many stars! They filled the sky from end to end, with wisps of celestial matter between. Only the tall trees around the edge of the village stood full dark against the starry expanse.

Then the breeze brought a whiff of corn and onions, complete with the hiss and pop of oil in a hot pan, plus a few more savory scents I didn't recognize. My mouth watered, but food alone wouldn't lure me out from under my warm blankets where, if I stayed long enough, maybe I'd get a bit more sleep.

No nightmares had visited me that night, but I lay still and awake for far too long. I'd thought the first night out of Philly silent, but now I knew better. Far worse to hear no traffic and no distant music and voices—but the rustle and call of animals and birds. A hoot here, a howl there, and for one while several shrill yowls and yips overlapping each other.

The owl I recognized right off, but the others had me freezing in place as I tried to figure out where they were coming from and whether near enough to try and get in. Hallemay and Grampa and I all got put up in a little two-room guest cottage with a thick door, but it was a little stuffy inside and Hallemay insisted on having the window ajar.

Grampa slept in the big double bed, only after Hallemay overruled his protests and near dumped him in. She took the single. As the youngest and halest, I got the pallet on the floor, which wasn't as bad as I'd feared. Particularly since Hallemay didn't snore this night.

I rolled over the other way, wrapping myself tighter in the blanket to escape the cool breeze wanting me to come out and play. Or so I guessed, for it kept slipping in and trying new ways of rousing me—and making me regret Grampa started teaching me to talk to breezes.

Maybe he could sleep through a breeze bringing ever

more bountiful breakfast scents. Or children calling words I didn't recognize. Light voices, mostly, older than Louie but not yet breaking into low and high. Bantering, I think, though only if that particular tone crossed language barriers.

Then the breeze blowing in the warm murmur of Hallemay and a deeper voice. An instant later, it brought images of her talking to the young man from last night as the two of them stood by her car. Then she placed her camera bag on the passenger seat, got in, and the car whuffled into a thrum as she drove off.

No, wait, that last sound I heard on my own even though muffled by the blanket. My belly jerked and grumbled as I sat up stock straight. Goose bumps covered my arms and shoulders. The bright yellow-and-red blanket pooled around my waist as I twisted to stare at the empty single bed.

Hallemay had up and gone, without me noticing.

The blanket she'd slept under last night sat tidily folded on a shelf along the far wall. The shelf bore a half-dozen other blankets in different color combinations, but I'd admired the lovely green-and-white pine motif on hers and wouldn't mistake it for another.

Wrapping the blanket around my shoulders, I rolled up the pallet and tucked it away under the bigger bed. Colorful braided rugs kept my feet warm, but I tiptoed across the cool floorboards between the rooms and at the window to the side of the door.

Gray clouds massed overhead. The breeze left me to go play with stronger gusts whipping limbs of the oaks and ash, and other trees growing in the village. Across a wide green expanse sat a row of houses visible through the trees. Painted all different colors—reds, greens, yellows—they were bright and cheery against the sky.

At the far end of the green, a dozen small figures surrounded a taller one. No doubt they'd played some kind of game, but now hurriedly gathered together before moving into a large building behind.

The car was gone.

As in—not there and nowhere in sight.

Hallemay had left me here. My breath seized in my throat.

A grumble from the other room, and I exhaled long and deep. Grampa was here too. I wasn't alone.

A few drops of rain pelted on the roof overhead, clanging when they hit the metal drainpipe of the cast iron stove. Turning, I scanned the room. All resembled my memory of the night before at first glance. Four small chairs around a table on one side, gleaming wood with a golden finish except for the signs of wear at the edges of the seats. Two armchairs upholstered in burnt umber on the other side of the room. A cold storage box in one corner. A closed cabinet painted cream in another. Bright yellow curtains at the windows. A large braided rug in the center, except where stones surrounded the feet of the stove.

The top of the stove had changed. Last night bare, now a piece of paper. It slipped through my fingers twice, landing under the stove the second time. The paper crackled as I finally unfolded it.

Grandfather and Mara,

I'm off on a job. Back soon. Breakfast'll be delivered. If you go out, don't go far. We'll leave by noon.

And Grandfather—get past Vesuvius with Mara, because it will make our stop in Georgia easier to explain.

Hallemay

Early as it was, I took a risk and called home.

Mom answered and brought me up to speed fast. She'd had a productive day at work and gotten a big tip. Louie mostly behaved himself, though he now knew not to try and paint the neighbor's cat. Since she planned to take him over for a cousin's birthday party, she didn't have long to talk.

So I asked a question pretty bluntly.

"Did Dad ever say anything about Grampa?"

"Is there a problem?"

"Not exactly." I traced the path of a raindrop rolling down a window. "I was just wondering."

"Your father didn't talk about his family much." A heavy sigh practically ruffled my hair, despite the long distance between us. "He was an only child. His mother died long ago, when he was young, and his father wasn't always around when he was growing up. That's about all I know, except that he grew up in Spain."

"That's what I know. Knew. Before Grampa . . ."

"Mara, are you okay? Is there something wrong?"

"No." I shook my head, trailing another drop. "No, it's not anything bad, just . . . Grampa started telling me about why he and Dad didn't get along. He's not saying anything bad about Dad, yet. But I get the sense Grampa and Hallemay think Dad was at fault."

After a long pause, she sighed again.

"You know I can't be impartial about your dad. He and I saw a lot of things differently. That said, he was a good man in most ways. He didn't lie or run around on me. He just couldn't stay in one place for too long. The worst I can say about him is he made a bad enemy. He knew his rights, and heaven help the person who tried to steal from him. And he loved you from the first, I never doubted that. Does that help?"

"Yeah." Closing my eyes, I imagined him standing before me. Every time we met, he'd stand with a quirky half-smile, then bend down and opened his arms for me to run into.

Mom's description didn't match that all the way, but close

enough. Easier to accept than Dad as a man ashamed and running away from his father rather than face that shame.

A thump in the other room caught my attention, and we ended the call.

Grampa hadn't fallen from the bed, but his cane had slipped and rolled out of his reach. He leaned on me a moment as he got out of bed, then grabbed the cane, and moved stiff as he passed into the small bathroom at the back. I used the time to get dressed in jeans, a green T-shirt without any decoration, and then I pulled on a light sweater after donning my socks and shoes. I left my hair down to keep my neck warm.

My stomach growled. I looked in every cabinet, crook, and cranny but found nothing except glasses and a pitcher of water from Hallemay's car. Filled with water from the tank in the back, of course. I filled a glass and drained it. That helped fill me up a bit, but I was still hungry.

A knock on the door had me freezing in place. Then, shaking my head at the foolishness, I opened the door to find the young man from the night before standing on the stoop. It extended just far enough to keep the rain off his head and torso. With both feet on the ground, he stood about my height so the first thing I noticed were his dark eyes—and hesitant smile.

Late teens, maybe, although who could know? Anyone guessing my age from my looks would be wrong, after all.

He wore his hair loose down past his shoulders so it trailed over his black-and-blue plaid shirt. His jeans chimed as he shifted his weight from one booted foot to another. From the looks of it, he had lots of keys or something stuffed in one pocket. He had medium brown skin, darker than Grampa and lighter than Hallemay.

His outstretched hands bore two covered plates.

The breeze winding around me strayed long enough to

bring back whiffs of onions and peppers. It also ruffled his hair, which made him shake his head.

Nodding, he said something in a language I didn't understand.

"Um, hi." I waved one hand and stepped back to let him in as a gust of wind blew rain through the door.

"Hi, you're Mara, right? Hallemay's little sister?" He switched to English.

"Yeah, I guess. That's what she calls me, anyway."

"Hmm." He tilted his head to one side, and light flashed on the rings dangling from his ear, silver against the dark strands. "I can see it. Something about the eyes and the set of your head."

"I guess." I shrugged, my cheeks heating at the indication he'd looked close enough to see a resemblance. "Who're you?"

"Jesse." The hesitant smile burst into full view, complete with a dimple on the left, before vanishing in an instant. "I noticed you peering out the door earlier, so I've brought your breakfast, still hot. May I?"

He headed right for the small dining table. With efficient movements, he laid out the plates and provided cutlery and napkins from a bag stuffed in his pocket. No doubt the source of the jingling. We'd brought our own water, of course, but he seemed to know where it was kept and ensured full glasses accompanied each setting.

Clumps and grumps marked Grampa's arrival. He stopped next to me, frowning at Jesse.

"Who's this?" He poked me.

"Jesse." I shrugged. Ducking my head as the manners Mom tried to instill in me registered, I continued the introductions. "Jesse, this is my grandfather, Ignacio de Leon."

"Please to meet you. I've brought food." Jesse finished setting the places and nodded at Grampa then me. "I hear you're traveling with Hallemay. I didn't know she took passengers."

"Not often, so far as I know." Grampa nodded. "But we're family. And this is an exceptional time. I am going home, and this is likely my last trip." Leaning heavily on his cane, Grampa walked over and sat at the kitchen table.

"I am sorry to hear that."

"Time catches up with us all, sooner or later."

Jesse nodded, then tilted his head and quirked his eyes my way, an unspoken question of some sort in them.

Maybe. I didn't know him, and I'd never been very good about guessing what went through other people's heads. But it seemed as though he wanted to know why we were traveling with Hallemay, even though he hadn't exactly asked as much.

"I'm just along for the ride." I shrugged. "I've never seen Grampa's home before."

"You will love it, I hope." Grampa leaned back in his chair, eyes closed. "There is no place under the sun to match it. Tall, ice-capped mountains in the distance. Long vistas across deep ravines, and canyons in every direction. The River cutting down from the mountains to the north. And above it all, the last remnant of the volcano that once birthed the land still stands watch."

For a moment, a breeze blew just such a scene before my eyes . . . until Jesse's voice broke the spell.

"I look forward to seeing it." He nodded at us, Grampa first and then me. "If you'll excuse me, I have yet to finish packing. Then I'll be back."

"Packing?" I asked.

"Didn't Hallemay tell you? I'm her new apprentice."

A grin stretched his face wide, not that I had long to see it. He slipped away while my mouth hung open enough for a horde of flies to enter.

"I like that young man. He knows how to make an exit." Grampa grabbed his cane and poked the open door with the tip. It swung shut and the latch caught with a firm snick. "We'll do well together."

A hundred, a thousand, questions flooded through me. What did this mean for Grampa's quest to find Torres? Why did Hallemay take on an apprentice right now, and why Jesse? What was he even apprenticing to her for? Photography or pathwalking or her courier business?

"Did you know?"

"About him? No." Grampa settled at the table. "That Hallemay might pick up an apprentice to ride along with us? Yes, merely not the where, when or who."

I showed him Hallemay's note, and he harrumphed. Then again, he might've been letting out more grumps.

He pulled the cover off his plate, releasing the full odor of meat and corn and onions. My belly rumbled, and questions seemed less important than eating.

We didn't talk much as we ate. What went through Grampa's head was as mysterious as ever, but I reeled over the news of Jesse joining us. As Hallemay's apprentice. And Grampa had known but neither of them had warned me.

Grampa's chair squeaked constantly as he kept shifting, and he gave a big sigh as he traded it for one of the arm chairs, thankfully silent. I settled into the other, which squeaked once.

He waved Hallemay's note at me.

"Shall we?"

Rain streaked down the nearby window.

"Might as well."

"Now, where did we leave off?" He scratched his chin, now boasting a thin day's growth of white hairs. His eyes thinned to slits and he tilted his head at me.

"Fleeing from Seville and the Inquisition, going to the Netherlands." I gave him the prompt he so clearly wanted.

"Ah, yes. This cycle continued for many a year. Torres would take Rainbow and Spring with him and relocate somewhere and settle in, but eventually draw negative attention and have to pick up and move along. Sometimes they fled one step ahead of inquisitors, sometimes other sorcerers." Grampa shuddered, scrunching up his mouth as though sucking on a lime. "For Torres was not content with long life and youth. He sought to gather ever more power and therefore collected all manner of magical artifacts, whether genuine or fake."

"Aren't most magical artifacts fake?" I settled deeper into the chair as rain beat against the window.

"Well, I wouldn't say quite that, but you're close enough. Some magicians have bound virtue into items, turning them magic, but they don't tend to work the way their makers plan. They're rarely very powerful. I've got a sword of El Cid in the back of the car, now, that's basically a hunk of heavy metal in a form meant for killing." He frowned. "It might have some power, but I've never seen it."

"Wait." I bolted upright, and the chair legs squeaked as it rocked back and forth beneath me. "You've got what?"

"One of the swords of El Cid. Torres had it, might've stolen it, but that was before my time so I don't know for sure. How I wound up with it instead's a twisted tale." He waved a hand, still frowning. "We can get to that down the road. One long story at a time, after all. But I think it will come in handy when we catch up with Torres. I need something to kill him with."

I could've lived without the reminder the goal of this trip was murder. Justified, based on all I'd heard so far, but still the act of killing someone. Assuming Grampa managed to carry it off. Sword in one hand and cane in the other? That didn't sound too promising to me.

"But I digress. We were speaking of Rainbow and Spring, and Torres. They spent decades traipsing across Europe in pursuit of this artifact then that, and having various adventures and misadventures, but those don't relate to the main story, so we'll skip them."

He raised an eyebrow at me, but what was I supposed to say? Yes, let's drag this out longer, tell me everything you know? Or let's cut to the chase. What happened to Rainbow and Spring, why did you lose track of Torres, and what did you ask Dad that made him stay away? And all the other hundred thousand questions connected, but these most of all.

I kept my mouth shut. He stared at me for a couple of moments. Then he shook his head and reached over to run his fingers along the side of my head and tuck my hair behind my ear. His callused fingertips were warm against my skin, but I shivered all the same.

Dad used to do that. Three times each visit. When he arrived, he'd grab me into a long hug then pull back and tuck my hair as he studied me for how I'd changed. A second time when he'd decided to tell me when he would leave. And last thing before he went away.

I fumbled for my glass of water and swallowed, forcing the liquid past my thick throat. My eyes burned, but blinking hard a couple of times kept back any tears. They wouldn't bring Dad back, not even to scold.

"It's okay to cry." Grampa did the same with the other side, again the quick slip of fingers tucking my hair behind my ear.

"I'm fine." I shrugged. "Go on."

"Very well." He scowled for a little while, but settled back into the chair and the story anyway.

Now this incident which Hallemay asked me to relate took place in Italy, about 1600. There are some things you need to know about the intervening years. For amidst their many moves about Spain and Europe, some matters have changed between Rainbow, Spring, and Torres.

First, Rainbow and Spring ceased running away at any opportunity. They actually stopped this within a few years, for Torres always found them—and it did not take them too long to ascertain why. He shared in some of Spring's powers by virtue of the way he drank it. When it ran over ground, the spirit of the spring knew where its water flowed until all healing power had drained away or joined a greater body of water. Trapped in Rainbow's body, Spring and Rainbow knew where Torres was at all times, for he had never yet gone very far away. So too, he knew where they were.

There was also the matter that they knew when those around them were ill or injured, for Spring sensed hurt and pain, and sorrowed that it could be of little to no assistance.

Nevertheless, for a few decades, they tried to kill him. Hurting Torres went against Spring's powers, but they tried all the same. Alas, by the time they reached Italy they'd exhausted most possibilities. Poison did not work, nor stabbing with knives. Beheading might have worked, had they managed to sever head from torso in the first strike, but alas they only laid open his face. Nor did they find an appropriate way to betray him that would ensure his death or imprisonment but not theirs, because he was far too politic. Although they retained hopes to do so and plotted to try again should they find a new and more likely way.

A few times, they trusted others with part of their secrets and enlisted aid in escaping Torres, but these never ended well. Only once did their co-conspirators survive such an attempt. Rainbow and Spring desired freedom, but not at the cost of innocent lives, and ceased sharing their woes.

They chose instead to masquerade and pretend compliance. After a decade or two, they worked subtly on Torres and he began to train them. He kept most things secret, of course, for he trusted no one, but he allowed them to learn ever more languages. Latin, Greek, Hebrew. Persian. And to read and help him in his researches, perhaps even find a magical artifact which they might use to free themselves, none of which did.

And while this took place, they also pursued other avenues of hope.

Can you guess?

By now, I knew it was futile to ask how Grampa learned this. Even if Torres and Rainbow and Spring raised him, why would they tell him? He'd said something about a letter from Rainbow and Spring. Must've been a very long letter.

I didn't guess. Didn't have a clue, not even when he leaned forward and flicked his finger against my water glass.

Then took a deep draft from his own, sighed, and shook his head.

Rivers, springs, brooks. Lakes and ponds.

The water spirits of Europe.

Spring and Rainbow sought them out, seeking assistance. Alas, they found none. They could not even communicate readily with the smaller bodies of water. Rainbow had not the calling gift. Although Spring taught her to speak with breezes, the spirits of air did not manage to whip any spring, brook, or pond into a frenzy to aid Rainbow and Spring.

Even the great rivers in Europe had no great mass of spirit. They were splintered, weakened by the extent to which the lands along them were fixed in place and did not move. Sometimes, with great rains, they managed to overturn matters and remind humans of their true power and might—but mostly they had to content themselves with undermining banks and seething in eddies.

They heard Spring's pleas, but passed her by and told her ever to seek more help further down-stream.

And this was the state of affairs when Torres betook himself to Rome, for a pilgrimage and to see what treasures he might find.

With him came Rainbow and Spring, dressed as a boy and masquerading as Torres's assistant. As such they were occasionally invited to attend him at banquets and dinners, although they were always seated far from the high tables, served last and least, and given the worst of the wines.

Yet this was a blessing in disguise.

For at one dinner, in a glass of wine, Spring detected the distant taste of water of life. Much reduced, of course, yet a faint tang remained. The vines must have been watered by a creek into which a spring of life ran. If Spring and Rainbow could only track it down, surely the other spring of life would aid them.

"Wait." I threw up a hand.

Grampa stopped fast and his lips twitched to the side in a half-smile. He must've expected I'd catch the second time through. The first passed so smooth by I barely noticed, but . . .

"There's more than one spring of life?"

"I don't know how many there are in all, but I would guess a reasonable number at the least. They're not unique, but require very specific circumstances attend their birth or creation since they are the melding of earth, fire, and water."

With perfect timing, rain lashed the window again. The pane rattled, but softer than before, perhaps due to a subsiding gasp of wind.

I refused to allow it to distract me, frowning and squirming in my chair.

"Then . . . why didn't Torres capture one in Spain?"

Grampa blinked and pulled back. His mouth gaped open for a moment or two, then shut with a click. A moment later he shrugged.

"Because there are none in Spain, to my knowledge. Don't ask where they are, but if I were to go looking, not that I am" —he fixed me with a sharp glare, definitely suggesting I not do so either—"I would focus on areas with the greatest volcanic activity."

"Got it."

"But back to Italy and our tale." He paused for a quick sip of water. "Skipping over tiresome details, it took Rainbow and Spring a number of discreet enquiries to ascertain the cheapest wines came from a vineyard on the river Sarno, near Mt. Vesuvius."

"As in Pompeii and Herculaneum?"

"Exactly. Which may give you some idea of how Rainbow and Spring convinced Torres to travel to Naples."

All fine and good, but some of the things I'd learned in school had stuck with me, and this didn't add up.

"You said this was a little after 1600. Pompeii and Herculaneum weren't uncovered until way later, weren't they?"

"In point of fact, I believe they were discovered in the mid-1700s, but a villa nearby was uncovered in 1590 during construction of a canal." Grampa smiled. "And so there were rumors of treasures around, and in the end that was enough to interest Torres."

Once based in Naples, Rainbow and Spring took every opportunity to scour the landscape for the spring of life. It required much time, for they had to conceal their labors from Torres, or find alternate reasons for their interest. Nevertheless, they persisted and eventually tracked down the vineyard. Studied the landscape.

Then, one warm summer day—not such as here and now, but in truth bright with a welcoming summer sun rising overhead—they ensured Torres was busy meeting with fellow collectors.

They hiked up Mount Vesuvius.

And tracked down the spring.

Although filled with excitement that they had found another spring of life, they had to find a way to communicate with it. Spring insisted relying on air spirits would not suffice. It needed to speak directly with the other spirit. But, imprisoned as it was within Rainbow's flesh, there was only one way to accomplish this.

To submerse themselves fully in the water.

Everything went so well until then. I'd listened to Grampa's tale. Heard it with my ears, but not any of my other senses. The breeze, or whatever pleased itself in dousing me with vicarious sensations, seemed to have gotten bored and blown itself off.

It blew back with a vengeance.

I froze as every pore in my skin insisted I'd jumped into water. Warm water rather than cold, or at least lukewarm, but that didn't make it any much better.

Water surrounded me. Everywhere. Absolutely everywhere! Pain bloomed as my mouth filled with water and the taste of blood. My throat burned.

Panic rippled through me, inside and outside, mine and not-mine. Memories of dying by drowning washed over me, rolling me within a wave I couldn't escape.

Except . . . warmth and ease, sorrow and companionship, and a touch of healing, followed.

My tight throat opened.

A trickle of water rolled down, carrying the faint taste of flowers. A warm arm curved around my shoulders, holding me against a strong chest.

"Just a little more." Grampa and I knelt on the floor, me within his embrace and him holding a glass of water to my lips.

I swallowed, letting the water carry away the last drops of blood and cleanse my sore lip where my teeth had nearly pierced through.

"Enough." I pushed the glass away.

"Better now?" Setting it down on the floor, he kept his arm around me. He brushed my sore, dry eyes with a finger and grunted, then dipped his hand in the remaining water and painted drops along my eyelashes. It didn't burn, instead leaving my eyes moist and well.

"Yeah. I don't know what that was. How to describe it."

"It's all right. I've done this before." He tucked my hair behind my ear again. "I've asked the breezes to leave you be awhile. That should do, until they forget. Somethings are better not shared."

"Okay." I shivered as a brief gust of cool air passed along my arm, and huddled a little closer to him. "Did the other spring help?"

"It thought it could break the spell." Grampa leaned his head against mine and sighed, onion-scented breath wreathing around us for a moment.

"Thought?"

There was a catch. There's always a catch. Or two or three. If the other spring broke the spell, Spring—our Spring, Rainbow's Spring—would join the spirit of the other spring and flow along the slope of Vesuvius for eternity. Or as close as makes no difference. Rainbow would be freed, but whether she would live and be able to make her way home or die in the attempt, the other spring could not be sure. For it would be focused upon Spring.

Neither Spring nor Rainbow were willing to take the chance. Rainbow would have agreed, had Spring wished it, because she wanted Spring to be free, although she would prefer not to die away from her native land.

Equally, Spring had no desire to join with the other spring— because it belonged in its birthplace.

They declined the offer with regret, and left with only the other spring's good wishes. With determination struck anew, they vowed to find a way to escape Torres faster than he could track them.

And return to their rightful homes.

He stopped there, just sat back and twiddled his thumbs with a distant expression on his face.

And no more explanation. They could've been free.

Torres wouldn't have gotten smacked down as he deserved, but he'd have withered and died and they'd have been free. Grampa's explanation for why they said no made no sense. I rubbed my temples, shaking my head.

"What has you so wound up?" He clucked his tongue at me.

"Why didn't they . . . why?"

"You grew up in Philadelphia. Do you want to be buried there?"

"What does where I'm buried matter?" I stomped over to the table, arms crossed. The smell of our breakfast lingered, at least the onions, but my stomach gave only a token growl.

"You are not part of Philadelphia the way Spring and Rainbow are the land of their birth. For them, the separation was as though they had . . . left part of themselves behind. To stay in Italy would mean forever being incomplete. To perpetuate the effects of the theft of them for the rest of their existence. To be free, they had to not only separate but be able to return home."

It still didn't make sense to me, not that I bothered trying to get any more from him. He understood, I didn't, that was all.

Except, somewhere deep within me a thread snapped or a string on a musical instrument twanged, and for a few moments my body thrummed with a deep, irresistible longing for a place I'd never been, never set foot—and yet every mote remembered existing at one with the earth and air, fire and water, only to have that reft away. Then the sense of place vanished.

But not the soul-splitting agony of losing that oneness.

FATHERS AND MEMORIES

$\mathcal{A}$ fourth person in the car changed everything. Physical differences registered before anything else. The actual act of fitting four people in, plus assorted bags and the water tank, which hadn't shrunk much despite all we were drinking, made for too much stuff plus people versus too little space.

Which made for too much heat, made worse by the thick humidity, although the rain lessened to a mere drizzle. The wipers squeaked as they brushed back and forth over the windshield, easily keeping up with the ooze.

Of course Grampa got the passenger seat back now the big, odd parcel had vanished. He turned up the air condition-ing, but the fans were in front and it took a long time for cool air to reach the back. The breezes abandoned me, although one danced around Grampa, lifting and twisting his white hair above the head rest. A layer of sweat ran down my back from neck to tail bone, dampening my T-shirt and making it stick to the textured cloth of the seat back. My legs oozed sweat within my jeans, making me wish I'd changed to shorts before leaving.

At least there were fewer packages in the back seat since Hallemay's delivery run. All the same, Jesse's bag filled one-third of the seat between us. It was an odd-shaped leather duffle, with the leather worn at the handle and ties. A beaded pattern in red, black, yellow, and green adorned the center, with no beads missing. The bag didn't smell of leather, but of wood smoke and a tinge of sweat.

Jesse had pulled his hair back into a thick braid, and had a few drops of sweat across his forehead, but otherwise didn't seem to notice the heat and humidity too much. Then again, he was no doubt used to it.

He made for a much more comfortable passenger in some ways, because he sat pretty still—back straight and boots planted firmly on the floor. Grampa, on the other hand, kept rapping his knees with his hands, tapping his feet on the floor, or shifting or jiggling some part or other. He needed to keep his blood flowing, but all the same I was glad to have Grampa back in the front and someone steadier on the seat beside me.

Plus, I liked having someone else young in the car. Someone else to talk to. Maybe.

Even after we turned enough corners the village went out of sight, and all his family with them, he kept casting backward glances. He'd had many, five to ten times the number who'd seen me off back in Philly, plus a couple of dogs, too. It made for quite a scene, with folks calling, some crying, and one of the little dogs, dark brown with a graying muzzle, whining until Jesse bent and gave it a hug.

All to be Hallemay's apprentice—as a pathwalker and maybe courier.

This proved to make them as irritating as the heat and humidity and Grampa's incessant shifting, just in a different way.

Because they talked to each other in some kind of code.

Whenever we reached a stopping point, Hallemay asked him to choose between two options. Only two ever, not more, even the time we came to a weird intersection of two straight roads plus an extra one so there were four possible ways to go other than turning around, something Hallemay never offered.

No matter what he said, and whether or not she followed his suggestion, she asked him why and he'd respond in ways that made little sense.

So the whole afternoon was filled with little exchanges such as when we hit a fork in the road.

"Right or straight?" Hallemay asked.

"Straight," Jesse said.

"Why?" She went that way.

"I didn't like the smell of things."

"Hmm."

Then we came to that weird intersection and she only asked, "leftmost or rightmost."

He chose left.

She asked why, again.

"Too many pigeons."

"Look a little harder." She went right instead.

At the next intersection, she gave him a choice between left and straight.

He picked left again.

She asked why.

"The sunrise."

This made no sense because the sun wasn't rising, but overhead. Further, going straight took us west, not east. All the same, Hallemay liked that, because she told him "good choice" although she usually kept her responses to hmms and nods.

I didn't follow anything else they said any better than that. So much for having someone else to talk to.

The whole thing wasn't too much of a hardship while we traveled rural areas without too many turnoffs and crossroads. Sometimes she didn't even ask him, just went whichever way she wanted.

But when we came to a city of sorts, my head ached with all the this way, that way, weird reasons. I'd have rather they'd talked in a different language because I wouldn't have understood much less, and I wouldn't have had the illusion I could figure out what they meant if I could only crack a code that I didn't really care about except when it was dangled in front of me.

So at the first opportunity, I tried to get Grampa to give me another installment of the story. I could handle it. I'd made it through the last one okay, basically. Plus, the breezes were staying away from me, no matter how hot that made things.

Epic failure.

And not even for any reason I could understand!

The rain stopped and the clouds parted to let bits of sun shine through. We made it past the city into another rural stretch with few real turnoff options. Some Hallemay didn't even bother offering Jesse a choice at. Which meant Grampa wouldn't be talking over them much.

I did all the set up. Explained to Jesse that Grampa had been telling me a long story to lighten the long drives and would he mind if we caught him up so Grampa could finish it for me?

Piece of cake.

Jesse didn't mind at all. Gave me a grin and said he loved stories.

"I'm sorry, Jesse." Grampa shook his head. "Mara, I should've told you. This is a special story. It doesn't belong to me, and I only have permission to share it with my family."

"Of course, sir." Jesse nodded his head.

Wait, what?

He understood. Grampa understood. Hallemay understood, for she too nodded.

As if they all shared some secret, but not me.

Which left me hanging in the wind with my request out there.

"I just thought it would help. You know, if Jesse knew then . . . then . . . well, when we catch up with Torres," if, not when, but no need to say that, "he can be backup."

"Good point," Hallemay said.

Grampa turned around in his seat and gave me a wide-eyed glance for a moment. Then his eyes narrowed and his head bobbed up and down as he looked Jesse over. Maybe noting the strength of arm and leg that Grampa didn't have as much anymore?

"Very well. I'll ask permission to share with Jesse, although I can't guarantee it will be granted."

And that was that for the three of them. No one said another word about the matter.

Especially since we'd reached another city with the attendant code-talk back and forth between Hallemay and Jesse.

The code-talk seemed partly to be about what each of them saw in the choices at any given turning, and whether whatever they saw—or heard or smelt or felt—was positive or negative. Maybe? But what they sensed, I didn't.

So I tuned out.

Just leaned my head back and let bits of sun stream down on me through the windows to make me sweat even more. Stretched out my feet as much as I could, despite how crowded the car still was.

And let my mind wander back . . . to my last trip with Dad before he died.

He took me to New York City, where I'd gone once before, when my school class went for a day and Mom had the money for the fare and fees. Then again, that time was in a crowded school bus on the Great Roads to the Metropolitan Museum and back again.

Dad took me by train. We left early in the morning, with the air crisp enough I didn't protest Mom making me wear a jacket. He hailed a bike cab down to the station, then we waited underground with all the sleepy business folk and travelers. Lots of them, in clumps here and there along the platform, but Dad kept my hand in his big, warm one and we promenaded to a place he declared just the right spot.

The train arrived with a hoot and toot, then slowed to a crawl as it inched along the platform. A door wound up right in front of us. Dad had the luck. Almost every trip with him, as far back as I remembered, he'd pick the right place to stand, get the best seat. Until that last time, when his luck ran out and the plane went down.

But I didn't want to remember that.

On the train, we had room and could stretch out or go walking up and down through the cars. So much better than a crowded bus. At eleven, I knew better than to run, though I had to resist temptation.

There was a dining car, too, though we didn't eat there because Dad had plans.

He always had plans.

Mom was left behind. She'd got up and let me out the door after giving Dad a run down on things I shouldn't do or eat. But she let me go with him, which she didn't always, because for once he'd called ahead and made plans with her rather than just sweeping into town and wanting to take me somewhere far away and then settling for an afternoon at the batball park or museum or such.

He was all about movement, shades of Grampa always twitching and pulsing with energy. Then again, he made the trip fun with stories and anecdotes and puzzles at every turn.

When we got to the city, he picked a bike cab for a special tour of the downtown—and put the tour guide through the wringer by asking every question imaginable about how the city had grown and changed over the years, stumping the guide more often than not. Most of the tour turned into a blur, but the sound of Dad's teasing voice resounded in my ears across the years.

Then we took a steamboat around the harbor and up and down the river. Well, technically a syngas boat, but the stacks still blew great gouts of steam without any coal debris. Dad got us a spot up at the bow, where the spray sparkled in the sun as it spritzed us. He pointed out all the buildings we'd seen from bike-back, now shining at different angles.

Lastly, dinner atop the highest building with all the city laid out below, slowly turning to little more than pinpricks of light against the growing dusk. White cloths on the tables, two layers of them, which I'd never seen before. No silverware or plates laid out until we got served. I don't actually remember what I ate, only that I ordered a special of the day at Dad's urging, and followed it up with a slice of the darkest, most decadent chocolate cake ever—which kept me up all the ride home.

He drank wine. I got sparkly water.

"Never settle for anything less than the best, for you deserve it." He toasted me, lifting his glass high. "The world didn't give me anything without making me fight for it. I want better for you. So seize hold and never let go. Don't let anyone take anything away from you. You're already and always a winner in my book."

A few hours later, he returned me home, with the chocolate finally wearing off. I stumbled into to a dimly lit apartment still smelling of the cabbage our next-door neighbors had cooked for dinner two nights ago.

He took half the brightness of life when he left.

HALLEMAY'S HOME

A jerk snapped my torso forward, until the seat belt dug into me. The bag next to me slid forward, then we both flopped back. The smell of leather and sweat filled my nostrils and dispelled the remembered cabbage, a trade I took without complaint. My body adapted to the shifts, still loose and languid from memory.

Grampa grumped from the front. The seatback shifted as he reached a hand around to rub his neck.

On the other side, Jesse's jaw gaped open. His eyes were wide as he turned his head this way and that along the road.

Didn't seem anything special to me. Fences lined the road to either side, rails of wood stretching forward and back. On one side grew trees in rows, the trunks stretching up to spread into countless branches supporting green leaf canopies. Small objects peeped through the leaves here and there, fruit of some kind though I didn't know enough to say what. Peaches, maybe, or apples.

Similar rows filled the land as far as the eye could see on the other side, but instead of trees vines dangled over wires.

Very pretty, all green and verdant and dusted here and

there with glittering drops of water that caught the sun and sparkled for miles. All the same, no lovelier than the woods and hills of Jesse's home, and not worth gaping at.

The car sat on the shoulder right next to the turnoff for a narrower road. More vines continued on the other side, and the same fences lined the other road until it dropped on the far side of a rise. A pole rose next to the intersection, with street signs on it. One I could read although it faced half away from me, obviously for the road we were on, while the other was blurry—though it should've been the clearer one.

"Sorry about that." Hallemay shook her head. "I almost overshot. Not used to so many passengers."

She opened her door. A wave of warm, humid air swept in carrying the hum of bees and growing things. The breeze that had danced in Grampa's hair dashed out to join others.

The car rocked as she got out. She stretched, back cracking, and shook her head until her braids jangled. Turning around, she slid her seat forward.

"Grampa's been here before and received guest privileges so he doesn't need an introduction, but you two do."

Jesse slid out without much problem. I had to squeeze around his bag, which was stuffed full and heavier than lead as I tried to shove it to the side. My hands ached as I finally slipped through the gap only to stumble as I exited the car.

Hallemay caught me before I could fall forward. Her hands braced me until I got my balance. Then she lined me up next to Jesse on the far side, shoulder to shoulder, facing the narrow stretch of grass between the car and the vineyard.

"Touch the ground." She knelt herself, placing both hands against the grass.

Jesse started before me, bending over. I was a beat behind and heard a hiss as his palms met the earth.

A second later I followed suit because something bit me. Hard. On both hands, in the fleshy part of the palm below the thumb. I jerked back. Small, slight pink welts marred my skin, but vanished a moment later.

Jesse wasn't so lucky. Bright red welts the size of a quarter, without any sign of teeth, rose above the surface of his hands. They took three or four times as long to fade as mine.

"It's different now." After one glance at his hands, he studied the horizon. A puzzled look crossed his face.

"Yes." Hallemay nodded. "The land will recognize you. Your people turned your home sideways to guard it, mine chose a different way."

In a matter of moments, we were back in the car and Hallemay had turned off to the side. She and Jesse started jabbering back and forth in their code-talk about turning the land at angles versus creating barriers or hiding in shadows.

As we passed the street sign, I could read the second half now. We traveled down North Safe Street, and there was a little tree etched at the end of the sign with a drawn shadow.

Hallemay broke out of the code-talk long enough to catch my eye through a glance back and then hold it through the rearview mirror.

"I'm taking you somewhere special: the North Georgia Sanctuary Territory. Mara, I've given you guest privileges, but you won't be able to return to the territory on your own if you leave. And Jesse," she shifted her gaze to him through the mirror, "you have temporary courier rights. You'll need to petition through the land when you return."

It took a few minutes for what she'd said to register, at which point I nearly lost my breath. There were so many states and self-governing territories in the nation it was hard to remember all the names. The North Georgia Sanctuary, sometimes called NOGA, was one of the best known and even I knew a little of its story. It started as a secret hideaway among the hills for people escaping from slavery, who couldn't go farther. The land itself sheltered the escapees and concealed them from slave owners and slave catchers. After the Civil War, the inhabitants expanded their land claims to include nearby plantations. They might have had to give it back, or fight, except the great change came and cemented their control. The Revised Constitution recognized NOGA as a founding territory, and granted it representation in the Reconstituted Congress.

It didn't look too different, yet. We drove down a road between farms and vineyards, all green and glowing with growth. Through a small village little more than two dozen houses around an intersection. On and on, as we wove around the low spires of a small city to another village on the far side.

Hallemay and Jesse had slid back into their code-talk at the intersection, but once we'd passed it, I interrupted a pause to ask how she'd gotten access to the territory in the first place. How long ago. Thinking she'd tell me about when she was an apprentice.

"I wasn't born here, but this is where I grew up," she said instead. "Whenever I'm able to stay off the road for long, I come back. My road always passes this way sooner or later. I don't have a home here anymore, but my daughter does.

"And that's where we'll stay."

There wasn't time to ask about local guesting practices, because Hallemay pulled up next to a cluster of buildings at the edge of a small town and came to a stop. Fences stretched out to either side, but here they contained vegetable gardens and chicken coop on one side, with more vines on the other.

Three houses formed a curve around a central parking area with two light trucks and two cars. The center house was the largest, with a second floor; to either side lay smaller cottages. Light gray smoke wafted up from narrow chimneys, along with the faint scent of cedar wood and sweet blossoms I didn't recognize.

Before I could absorb much more, a young girl appeared in the doorway and screamed at the top of her lungs. "Auntie Hallemay's back!"

Two older men, one with white hair and the other gray, came around the side of the house with a woman and a small boy.

The car door swung open and Hallemay emerged to be swallowed up in hug after hug. Everyone exclaimed over her being just in good time, they were doing fine, just napping, did you bring it, have you got it, and other variations.

"Good to see you back again!" After hugging Hallemay, the white-haired man went over to Grampa and gave him a hug and back slap. "One of these days you let me in on your secret because you don't look a day older than when last I saw you."

The girl, about Louie's age in a lime green dress over yellow shorts, clambered into the car and half-way atop Jesse's bag.

"Who're you?" Thick box braids sprang from her sepia skin, all ending in gold and purple barrettes that rattled as she glanced back and forth between me and Jesse. "Mama said Auntie was bringing family and an apprentice. Which's which?"

The girl was Rayla, she told me as she helped me get out of the car, where help meant talk while backing very slowly out of the way.

I didn't have a chance to introduce myself. Jesse squeezed out after me and told Rayla he was the apprentice and I Hallemay's little sister.

Rayla's mama's brother'd married Hallemay's daughter Mayanna, Rayla said, and decided I qualified as Auntie, too. This made her giggle, a lot, because she was nearly as tall as I. She introduced me as such to the other child, her little brother Jordy. He had his hair cut short on the sides but rising to a high, flat top giving him at least five additional centimeters in height to come close to matching his sister.

Everyone seemed to be talking at once, and to everyone. Which of course wasn't the case, but the whole thing reminded me of the first day of work at a new job, when I didn't know anyone but the manager who'd hired me—to bus tables my first job, wait on them second—and hadn't a clue where anything belonged.

When I didn't belong.

I kept my back to the car, one hand wrapped around the frame, as the children buzzed around me. The adults glanced over, then a full hush fell. From several talking to none in the space of a second.

The front door of the house opened and three people walked out. First a youngish man, tall and lithe, and then an older woman. Both wore jeans and blue shirts, and had short black curls, hers streaked with gray. Mother and son, at a guess, and with kind faces. They took great care of the other woman, who held onto their arms so tight that her warm mahogany skin turned gray at the knuckles.

The younger woman stood a head taller than the older woman, almost as tall as the man. Millimeter-short strands of hair revealed the oval shape of her skull. Thin layers of bone and muscle formed her limbs, which trembled with each step. Her yellow dress hung loose about her except at the middle where it strained taut over her pregnant belly.

She had Hallemay's face.

Hallemay crossed the distance in a few long strides. She took her daughter in a gentle embrace, and a moment later the two of them moved inside the house. The older woman remained outside calling for the others to gather jugs and bottles.

"This way." Grampa's hand fastened on my shoulder.

I jumped, not having heard him sneak up behind me. His

fingers dug deep, then released. With a flick of his cane, he directed me and Jesse to start unloading the car's wayback. He supervised, leaning against the side of the car. Bags and suitcases went to sit at his feet until eager hands snatched them up and carried them away.

On the other side, a pile of empty milk jugs and gallon bottles accumulated with clangs and thuds.

"Fill them up." Grampa rapped the water tank tap with his cane. "Pour out at least half what remains."

Jesse and I near tripped over each other until he insisted I work the tap while he held the jugs and bottles below. The faint floral scent of the water managed to obscure all other smells, this close to the tank.

Which earned an approving nod from Grampa.

Bossy, but it wasn't worth fighting over. I wasn't sure why Jesse was so quick to jump to Grampa's orders, though he did without so much as a second glance or rolling of his eyes.

Both of which I did, once only. Then Grampa leaned in and laid his hands atop mine, fingers cool despite the general heat.

"Give. It's for Hallemay's daughter."

I lost count of how many containers I filled, each one whipped out of Jesse's hand and carried carefully over to the far cottage. At least it gave me something to do, a purpose, and a way to avoid all the eyes that might be watching me.

The tap didn't speed up past a moderate flow, no matter how I cranked it.

The man who'd walked out Hallemay's daughter swapped with Jesse, and the gray-haired man took my place. He couldn't get the tap to work any faster, but I stepped back to stand at Grampa's side and watch the circle of people carrying water into the cottage.

"Why're we doing this? Don't they have running water?"

"Yes, but not such as this." He gave me a strange look. "I'd have thought you'd have figured it out by now. This is water from a spring of life."

"From a spring . . ." I should have guessed, and yet why? "But you said, back when you started the story, that the spring's water weakened with distance."

"So you were listening." He wrapped an arm around my shoulder, leaning into me. "True, the water's power to heal dilutes to nothing the farther away from the source. Still, if drawn with the spring's consent, the water can strengthen bodies and support natural tendencies towards health. As a courier, Hallemay knows people who know people who have access to springs of life, and allow her to carry some where her road takes her."

"Water of life." Jesse wiped a layer of sweat from his forehead. Turning away from the bustle, he retrieved from the car the bottles we'd been drinking from on the way. Grampa took his and set it aside. Jesse drank deep.

I took a sip, letting the faint sweet and savory taste swirl around my mouth before I swallowed. Didn't feel any different after, except maybe not quite so hot and sweaty. Though a breeze blew by me, thinning the heavy, humid air, which helped.

Jesse and Grampa talked over my head about couriering water, but I heard only their voices and not the words.

The tank shrank as water flowed out. I'd seen this before, albeit in smaller measure. Back in Philly, when Grampa and Hallemay left some of the water at home for Louie.

Louie.

Who Mom had said was doing fine—active, healthy, no more allergy attacks.

Thanks to Grampa?

TURTLES AND ALLIGATORS

Surprise, surprise I wound up back at a zoo the next afternoon.

Sweet flowers I didn't recognize perfumed the morning air, but couldn't completely override the scents of the animals stirring. Most of the dew had already dried, and it promised to be hot later. At least we'd made it here early enough to enjoy the cooler air.

Grampa's suggestion, of course. We went to church with the family, except Mayanna and Hallemay who stayed with her. Then Grampa volunteered me, Jesse, and himself to bring Rayla and Jordy here and let the adults enjoy a quiet afternoon while reconnecting with Hallemay. At least, that was how I'd interpreted what he said, but he spoke in so many circles I wouldn't swear to it. Same difference in the end, because we wound up here.

And sooner or later Grampa'd wind up talking to alligators, but this time I was able to enjoy the big cats with two kids who didn't sneeze at a bit of cat hair.

One on either side, hanging off my hand and pulling me

in two directions at once, except which two directions kept changing as they pointed this way and that.

Although I hadn't mentioned dressing alike, same as whenever I took Louie out on my own, Rayla, Jordy, and I all wound up wearing blue. Rayla added gold and blue barrettes in her hair. My plain square-neck shirt still carried a little of the crisp, cheap detergent Mom used back home.

We tried to stay together. At least, I tried. I had experience wrangling one kid. Both Rayla and Jordy hung on me, rather than Jesse or Grampa, for some reason. Maybe because I was so close to them in height.

They spent an hour, at least, watching the big cats. Rayla loved the leopard while Jordy preferred the tiger. Which turned into a massive back and forth spat between "Spots!" and "Stripes!" until Jesse helped me convince them to follow Grampa to the reptiles or the slimy, scaly critters.

Where we found no alligators. Just an African slender-snouted crocodile floating in a fake pool.

Grampa had a lively discussion with it. His body contorted, eyes laughing within his warm bronze face as he emitted a series of high-pitched squeaks—which made Rayla and Jordy and other children visitors giggle—and the crocodile gave a bellow in return.

After a second round of squeaks, the crocodile raised itself partly out of the water and opened its mouth wide.

"How about those teeth!" I pointed at the gaping maw. "Can you count them?"

Rayla started, though Jordy got stuck on counting to four and starting over.

It kept them occupied as the breezes started sharing Grampa's conversation with the crocodile with me. Or so I assumed. After all, why else would the image of Torres flash across my eyes only to shift into an immense crocodile?

Grampa seemed to be asking how to fight it, which sure

was nosy of him since the crocodile lived in captivity. A very nice, large environment specially constructed for it, but still captivity.

The crocodile told Grampa to make himself look bigger. Hiss. Use his teeth.

Then a separate image of a pale, whitish underbelly flashed before my eyes. It wasn't from the crocodile, either. It had a different tang to it, and seemed to come from behind me.

Turning around and around until I got dizzy, I couldn't find any reasonable source.

Jordy'd given up counting, and slipped his hand into mine. His teeth flashed as they bit into upper lip. On my brother, that'd be a bad sign of an incipient temper tantrum. Just in case, I bent down and whispered to him.

"Let's go see what else we can find. We'll get there first."

He nodded. His soft fingers managed to keep a tight grip on me as we passed snakes and serpents, with their beady eyes tracking our progress. His short legs went fast by things that slithered, but slowed for the turtles and tortoises. Then stopped when we got to what had to be the granddaddy or grandmommy of all turtles.

A nearby sign proclaimed this an alligator snapping turtle.

It lay on the bottom, beneath the water, unmoving. Thick, short limbs of gray-green extended from a heavy shell. Two large nostrils topped a massive, triangular head with beady eyes no bigger than the nostrils combined.

Jordy crouched next to the glass.

Floating up slowly, it poked its nose out of the water for a long moment and then settled to float in the water. The turtle's mouth opened to show the tongue had a bright red section which wiggled as though it was a worm. Jordy giggled, tracing the movements with a finger against the glass.

At the same moment, the breeze brought to me a second image of a pale, whitish underbelly. Then sharp teeth chomped down. Blood sprayed as a larger alligator killed a smaller one.

I jerked back. Chills rippled up and down my spine.

The turtle stuck its nose above the water again.

A second vision of alligators fighting, a bigger one managing to flip the smaller and drive its teeth into the soft underneath. Along with the image came a sense of assurance, that this was the answer to the question.

"You heard Grampa asking . . ." I didn't want to mention killing with Jordy near.

The turtle just stared at me as it slowly sank down to rest on the bottom of the tank.

I didn't have a chance to tell Grampa then or at any time during the rest of the trip. Wrangling the children around the zoo exhausted me. Grampa, too, for he napped in the van Jesse had borrowed from Rayla's parents. The kids gave Jesse directions, but he managed not to get lost.

We got back early evening to hot, heavy weather.

No sooner had we gotten out of the van than the older woman I'd seen with Hallemay's daughter cut me off from the rest. She wore a loose dress this day, the same light shade as my shirt although the color looked better on her than me. I'd learned her name and identity the night before, and both came to mind after a moment's startlement.

Rochelle, the matriarch of the family and mother of Hallemay's daughter's husband, as well as mother or grandmother or aunt to nearly everyone else.

"This way." Her arm wrapped around my shoulder and fingers fastened on my upper arm. Light, but firm, as she guided me into the cottage where Hallemay's daughter and her husband lived. The small living room sparkled despite the curtains drawn at the windows to keep the hot sun out. A few pieces of art—intricate paintings of vines covered in grapes, an immense photo of a road lined with trees dripping red and gold leaves, and a portrait of a woman who might've been a younger Rochelle—hung on walls painted pale yellow. Several chairs lined an exterior wall along with a table with the sides folded down. A combination kitchen and dining room lay through an archway close to the front entrance. Doors at the far end lay open to offer glimpses into two bedrooms. One held a double bed and ample signs of regular use. The other was partly painted in the same yellow and held a half-assembled crib. The whole smelled of disinfectant and sage.

A single bed hugged the wall opposite the chairs, with Mayanna lying propped up by several fluffy pillows. Wide straps of orange stretched across each shoulder, and the top of her dress peeked out above the thin pink sheet drawn over her body. Her face seemed fuller than the day before, and her skin less gray.

Next to the bed, within arm's reach, sat a glass and a pitcher of water on a small wooden table.

Hallemay was nowhere to be seen.

"I don't think you've met. Mayanna, this is Mara. Mara, Mayanna." Rochelle twitched the end of one pillow and leaned down to brush a kiss across Mayanna's brow.

"My mother's little sister, and therefore my aunt." Mayanna stretched out both hands. Her long fingers had a thin layer of muscle over the bones. "She's told me so much about you, it's good to finally meet."

"Nice to meet you too." A squirrely sensation rilled through me at the notion of being someone's aunt, though I also flushed at hearing, again, that Hallemay called me sister behind my back as well as to my face. I put my hands in

Mayanna's, not daring to squeeze or do anything other than touch skin to skin. Hers was cool and dry, mine warm and a little sweaty. "I hope you're feeling better."

"Yes. The water helps. I have hopes all will be well this time." Mayanna withdrew her hands, both dropping to rest on her belly.

"From your mouth to God's ears." Rochelle filled the glass with water and handed it over.

Mayanna drank deep, in regular, even gulps. The muscles of her throat shifted with each swallow.

The sheet over her belly rippled with a side-to-side movement. Both women smiled at the sight.

"Would you like to meet your great-niece or nephew?"

"Okay?" The whole aunt and great-aunt thing had me somewhat in knots. I'd got used to having Hallemay as an honorary big sister, but hadn't realized it extended to the rest of her family. I couldn't quite imagine myself as an aunt yet, much less a great-aunt, but it was cool. Except, I hadn't come this near a pregnant woman since Mom had Louis.

Mayanna caught my hand and laid it atop. Something kicked at me. I leapt back, stumbling into the chairs lining the wall.

"You will have to come back after my child is born, and I am allowed out of bed." My niece, as it were, closed her eyes for a moment. Her lids fluttered, then she opened her eyes again and gave a speaking glance to Rochelle.

The older woman's mouth tightened, but she leaned down and kissed Mayanna on the forehead again.

"Don't tire yourself. Hallemay will be back soon enough. She always is." Rochelle laid her hand on my shoulder and gave a squeeze. "Five minutes, no more."

Then she was out. The door closed with a click behind her, and the room seemed suddenly smaller and darker. I settled onto the edge of the chair. It squeaked and rocked beneath me.

"I wish we could have talked more first." Mayanna sighed. "Instead I must ask you a favor."

"Do you want more water?" I grabbed the handle of the pitcher, the metal cool to the touch despite the general warmth, and nodded at the glass.

"Always, but I can poor my own." Mayanna shook her head, rolling a little so she faced me more squarely. "If you go out and down the lane, then turn left towards town, you'll see a school in the distance. There's a bench next to the school's front door, facing the houses across the street. If I'm not mistaken, you'll find my mother there. I'd like you to take her a message."

"Sure, I mean I'll do it. I just . . ." It seemed the wrong way around to send me to track down Hallemay, who'd be better at finding people. The request made Hallemay's absence more obvious, even as it was inexplicable. She'd traveled a long distance to bring her daughter water of life, for strength, and now she'd gone off for a walk?

"I'm asking you because the fact that I have chosen you to take the message, rather than Grandfather or my husband or Mother Rochelle," Mayanna cast a glance skywards, "means my mother is more likely to take my message the way I mean her to."

"All right." Though it wasn't quite, for I still didn't understand why she wanted me. All the same, the directions sounded clear enough. "You want me to go now?"

"Yes. Tell her I understand, I love Grandmother too, and I'm sure she'll be back in time." Mayanna also kissed my cheek with her cool lips, as one more thing to take to Hallemay.

The skin along my shoulders prickled under my shirt as I walked out of the cottage and down the lane. An almost unnatural quiet, except for the buzz of insects and the distant clatter of pots and dishes, accompanied with stray scents of apple pies cooling in a pie safe.

No one else moved about the yard, just like yesterday. Except a glance back showed Rochelle watching from the stoop of the largest cottage. Then she walked over to Mayanna's.

Gravel crunched beneath my feet, pebbles shifting and sometimes skittering over the road as I headed out.

I had no trouble following Mayanna's directions, though my skin prickled as I passed down the graveled lane towards town. Most of the houses, granted there weren't many, had at least one person sitting out on a porch or under a tree. All of whom glanced at me, stopped for a moment, then gave a nod or wave. They must have heard of my visiting, for no one challenged me.

But they watched.

The school wasn't far away, but the walk and heat, even in under the lowering sun, meant a light sheen of sweat made my shirt stick to my back and slicked my hair under my hat. The school itself was red with white trim, and built in stages. The center part had a brick foundation. The wings to either side sat on concrete, and the paint had also evidently been done in stages, because it had faded at different rates. In some ways it was more a pink and red school than red.

A row of cottages, none bigger than Mayanna's, lay across the road. Each had a small, fenced yard and was painted a different bright color. Red, brighter than the school, blue, yellow, green.

Just as Mayanna had said, a black bench sat in front of the school, under the shade of a big, old oak tree. Hallemay sat with her back straight, but her arms wrapped tight over her chest, fingers tucked under. Her yellow T-shirt was wrinkled and sweat-stained, and a long, loose blue skirt fell to her ankles, showing only the tips of her toes and sandals. A half-filled bottle rested by her feet. She stared at the blue house across the way. Didn't flicker an eye my way.

My mind a blank on how to start the conversation, I sat down next to her.

A light breeze blew around, kindly drying the sweat on my back but otherwise, for once, not tossing stray images, sounds, or scents.

"Did Rochelle send you?" Hallemay didn't move, but the breeze whisked her words to me clear as she'd spoken.

"No, Mayanna did. She says she understands."

"Yes. She always does." Hallemay's head drooped, and a half-sob escaped her though her eyes seemed dry. "God blessed me with the most wonderful, loving child I could have . . . and I keep having to leave her."

Neither of Mayanna's other messages fit, so I kept my mouth shut about them. On the other hand, I knew some of the basics about magical powers. Even those of us who didn't have them got taught bits and pieces in school.

Most powers were genetic: you either were born with one or you weren't. Although some gifts ran in families, they also cropped up unpredictably among people of every race, ethnicity, gender, and birthplace. The important thing was once you used your gift enough to "turn it on" as it were, turning it off became almost impossible.

"Does being a pathwalker make you have to stay on the move?"

"If I'd never used my power, I could stay in one place without problems—but once I started tracking, I had to keep on. Keep finding intersections and thus keep moving." She shook her head. "People call magical powers curses as well as gifts for good reasons."

"It's not your fault you can't stay. It's your being a pathwalker. Like you said, once you started, that was that. She knows."

"Once I started?" Hallemay gave a choked laugh. "Oh, there's irony in that, and cruelty. You want to know how I got started finding paths?"

The bench creaked and the slats vibrated as Hallemay leaned back. She closed her eyes and let her head fall forward. Her arms dropped to rest at her sides.

The tone of her voice suggested I'd regret asking, so I didn't. Except . . . maybe she needed to talk. Her hand lay near me, as long fingered as her daughter but with more muscles and flesh on the bones. I touched it with mine, wanting to do something but blank-minded. Her fingers twisted in an instant. She grabbed me and twined her hand with mine, holding tight.

"I was born before the War." She must've caught a puzzled look on my face. "The Civil War. I'm older than I look by a long sight, for our family live well beyond the usual century. Something you can look forward to."

The notion of living longer didn't catch my imagination much. Most people who lived past five had a good chance of living to be over a hundred, but I was only eighteen. Mom at forty seemed old to me, so the idea of someday being older was far off.

Rather, her clarification, and knowing she'd wound up here in NOGA and considered it her home, caused a lump of dread to form in my throat. I swallowed, having a guess and fear as to what she might have gone through.

My mother was enslaved on a big plantation, not that far from where we are nowadays but it was farther back then. Or seemed so. A white man passing through took a fancy to her, and she couldn't say no. That led to me.

All I knew my first years was the same as other enslaved children—keep out of the way of the white folks. Except, one of my earliest memories is of running and being stopped by a white man who held my arm and looked me over. Told me to lead him to my mother. Which I did.

The man turned out to be my father, passing through again. He did so more regularly after that. Didn't pay any mind to my mother anymore, but once or twice a year he'd stop by and want to see me.

He bought me, you see. Told me it was my freedom he'd bought, and I could have it when I was old enough to leave on my own. He didn't want the raising of me, though, so he paid my mother's enslaver good money to keep me healthy and well-fed and clothed, so I'd be fine when he next passed by.

He didn't buy my mother's freedom. Just me. When I was eight or so, there was talk among the people enslaved on the plantation that the enslavers weren't doing well. Run up debts they couldn't pay. I might not be sold, but my mother and brother and sister weren't safe.

I'd heard, most all had, about refuges, sanctuaries, where folks could run and if they got there no one could ever drag them back. Rumor said one was closer than fleeing north to freedom.

I wanted so much to find one. For me. For my brother and sister. For my mother, who'd been ill after losing a babe. Kept wondering, worrying at it, and then suddenly one morning I crossed an old track and knew if I turned left on it, I'd find a sanctuary. Felt it in my bones that I could lead us there.

It wasn't easy. I didn't have to convince anyone—they were all readier than me. Took us more than a week, but we made it.

And by the end, I'd become a pathwalker—to get my mother and siblings to freedom. Stepped on my road, and only once did I ever manage to stay off it for long.

When Mayanna was little, I had her with me on the road. Her father and I both did, until our roads parted. He's a pathwalker, too. We spend more time living without each other than with. We took turns with her, when our roads didn't run together, until it became clear she wasn't a pathwalker. That she wanted roots.

We talked, all three of us, and in the end I came off the road, came here, and stayed for a decade so she could have a place to grow and flourish. It was hard, staying in one place except for summers when we went back wandering, but I managed until I just couldn't any longer and Rochelle said she'd take care of Mayanna for me."

Hallemay gave a short, bitter laugh. "She still does.

Her grip had grown progressively tighter around my fingers. Tendrils of pain radiated up my arm, but they hurt less than the weight in my belly. And both together didn't amount to the smallest slice of what Hallemay must've gone through.

"I'm sorry."

She startled, as though she'd forgotten I sat so close, and let go.

"It was long ago."

"Doesn't mean the memory doesn't hurt. Or it isn't hard having to always be the one who leaves." I flexed my fingers gingerly and shook out my hand. That didn't seem enough on its own, so I put my arm around her shoulder. Slow. If she pulled away, I'd have stopped, but she leaned in and lowered her head to rest on my shoulder, let me hold her for a little bit.

"It is hard."

I rubbed her shoulder and gave her a hug, which she returned.

"You said Grampa helped arrange for supplies, when you first met him. Is this where he brought them?"

"We brought them," she corrected me. "Yes. The armies couldn't get into NOGA. No battles were fought on this ground. When Sherman burned Atlanta, though, the fires swept up here. By the time we put them out, we'd lost most of our supplies. I left to find what I could, and that was when Grandfather tracked me down. He hired a pathwalker, if you can imagine, to find his son and at the same time see if he had any kin he didn't know of, and that pathwalker located me. And Grandfather used every coin he had on him to see us fed and help us rebuild."

"He's that old, too?" Easier to imagine it of Grampa than of Hallemay, for some reason.

"Older. I did say our family lives long. If we die of old age, that is."

Which brought her daughter to mind, who might not live to die of old age.

"Mayanna's doing better, though. Since you brought the water."

"Yes, better, though there's no guarantee she'll be able to carry the child to term. I want to be here for her, but as always, my road is calling me away. I have to take you and Grandfather west."

I shook my head. The problem wasn't that Mayanna lived so near Rochelle and looked on her as a second mother, but that Hallemay had to go.

Or did she? She'd said her road called her away to carry Grampa and me, but if someone else could . . . "Surely Grampa would agree to having someone else take us, Jesse—"

"No, Jesse won't be ready to carry other folk on the road for a while." Hallemay gave a deep sigh and sat back up straight, shaking off my arm. "Oh, he can take little trips such as to the zoo, where his road aligns with those he's carrying, but it takes time to learn how to carry passengers on splitting roads. To make choices weighing one's personal road against the roads of those one's guiding, and if there's more than one passenger how to make choices between their roads. It'll have to be me. I'll see this through."

"Mayanna also said to tell you she loved Grandmother,

too. Or Grandfather." I wasn't quite sure which she'd said. "And that she believes you'll be back in time."

"One way or another." Hallemay stood, dusting off her skirt. "I'll take you on, but there are limits. You've got a week to find Torres and then I'm either leaving you in Santa Fe or you're on your own wherever you are."

"A week?" Her sudden reversal made me sit up stock straight, all hairs on end. I didn't blame her for wanting to stay here, but surely there were other options. "Grampa's been looking for him for years."

"Don't be fooled." She shook her head. "Grandfather may not know where Torres is exactly, but he's kept general tabs on him. He told me from the get-go, before we picked you up, to head for west Texas and I'd know more when we got there."

RUNAWAY

$\mathcal{M}$y feet pounded stone. Only a thin layer of shoe leather separated my flesh from the narrow, cobbled street. Each step reverberated up through my shins, legs, and torso. Pain flared—dying an instant later, a cycle repeated over and over. My skirts swayed, heavy with coins sewn into the hems which hit my ankles in the same spot every time. More pain, more repetition. I fought for every breath, dragging in the humid air and no doubt panting.

The morning sun didn't reach the street. All was different degrees of shadow. The cool air hung still. Buildings crowded in to either side, brick and stone walls rising two and three stories high. The roofs rose to high peaks above, tiled in slate or tin.

The streets should be full, yet they lay empty before me. Somehow I knew that once people of all manner and types thronged the narrow space. Venetian men in bright-colored doublets or coats over breeches, women in dresses with ruffs at the neck and full skirts. Turkish men in equally bright flaring kaftans. Catholic priests in dark robes, and soberly clad nuns.

Although I saw no one, my hands brushed evidence of their presence. I pushed through, past heavy brocade skirts, soft silks, and plain coarse burlap. This struck my dream self as wrong. I should feel costly fabrics or cheap, not both so close in the same street.

On I ran. Outward. Downward.

Wrongness hit me with every step. I tasted nothing, not even my own spit as I swallowed. I smelled nothing, not even my own sweat.

A blank filled my ears. So much I should hear—my footsteps, labored breathing, and if nothing else my heart pulsing in my chest.

Nothing.

One street, two, three, four. They all blended together, fading from one to the next without any clear memory of turning a corner or changing direction. I ran only forward.

Until the moment sound broke in upon me. Not my footsteps, breaths or heart beat—but dogs barking. Everywhere and every one. Little dogs yapping while bigger gave harsh, deep growls.

I stopped in the middle of the empty but not-empty street.

The next instant, the bells began to ring. Every one and everywhere. This was a city of bells, of churches and monasteries all ringing in a gigantic cacophany.

A sharp jolt made me sway in place. My weary legs gave way and I dropped to crouch on the stone street.

The movement paused long enough for me to recite an Ave Maria, a few seconds, maybe eight or ten but no more.

Then a second jolt.

Stones fell, houses crashed, buildings dissolved into heaps of rubble. I lost air, lost light, lost sight. Something fell upon me. I should have died, but I survived. Pain rippled through me, my own and that of those around me.

I don't know how long I lay beneath layers of brick and tin. Long enough for the crackle of fire to draw near. Smoke, heavy and thick, filled the air. Each breath dragged in ash.

But bricks shifted. Tin melted or slid away. I rose from the rubble bloody and bruised, but whole.

This was my chance.

And then everything changed. I stood aboard a ship, one row back from the railing. Bodies pressed in on me from every side, most shaking apart from the sway of the wooden deck as the waves rose and fell beneath us. The smells of smoke and sweat, and incense, filled my nostrils. The women around me wore plain habits, some black and others beige, their headdresses likewise different mixes of white wimples and white or black head coverings. A similar robe covered my gown.

Next to me, a nun wrapped her hands tight about my arm, shaking and near collapse. A dark bruise marred her right cheek, extending beneath her wimple. We'd met earlier, at the docks, where she'd straightened my attire for me— though she knew me not nor I her. Fellow sufferers drawn together in adversity.

"We are all that is left," she said, her voice low. "Though there were once three times our number in the city."

White sails were furled along the masts, for the winds blew against us and kept us in the harbor. Close enough to see smoke rising high as towns and cities continued to burn.

If only Torres burned with the buildings.

This was our chance. I was not singular but once again three-fold: Rainbow, Spring running in her veins, and me-Mara dreaming it all. All our hearts beat fast, blood pounding, as we made our break for freedom.

Or they did. Maybe.

The dream kept shifting on me. It shattered, somehow, so I dreamt only unconnected fragments.

From the ship's deck, I fell backwards in time to clamber over a ruined wall. Slipping past the dead, with their empty eyes facing the sky, I stole a habit from a fallen nunnery.

Then I stood on the bow of a different ship, in a boy's attire of loose breeches and a doublet. This shore glowed green and vibrant, although the countryside in the distance bore scars of strife. The air hung warm and thick with humidity. The sun shone far more fiercely overhead than before.

And switch and switch and switch.

As though I'd been fake nun, fake boy, fake well-born lady down-on-her-luck, fake serving maid, or any of a half-dozen masks all in turn, and all jumbled up.

Traveling by ship, on foot, in wagons.

Hearing voices in English, Dutch, Venetian, Turkish, Latin, and others—all of which I understood to some degree, although I-Mara rarely knew what anyone had said.

I was here, then there, then somewhere else.

All with relative freedom. In each mask, each location, each pretense, I kept to my part. Walked only where I might. Bargained and paid only what I must.

Yet traveled free of Torres and untrammeled.

Until a shift dropped me into a hot, stifling room. Shackles bound my wrists together. An unnatural position, this strained arms and shoulders. I healed and hurt, hurt and healed. Chains weighed down my feet as well, draping from my ankles. Other bodies crowded closer around me than aboard ship, all likewise laden down. A stench filled the air, part urine and feces, part sweat and tears, part fear and anger.

Then all senses vanished save hearing. A voice rose and

fell in the unmistakable cadences of an auctioneer touting the latest item for bid.

Torres' face burst into view. His hair had lightened, gray streaking through the black. Wrinkles webbed his temples and brow. A livid scar, pulsing and red, stretched from mouth to ear.

His hand wrapped around my wrist. The shackles fell away. Something sharp broke skin and veins, and pain blossomed as once again he drank deep.

He lifted his head, lips and teeth stained with my blood, and smiled.

I scrambled to get away, but he held tight. His arms pinned mine against my chest. No matter how I wriggled and writhed, I couldn't slip free. I tried to lash out, but somehow he held my shoulders down against the ground.

"You'll never get away," he said. "You're mine for always. Ssssssss."

My heart pounded faster than ever, breath coming in pants, as I braced for one more attempt to throw him off.

Yet in that silence, the hiss changed to "Sssh. Sssh."

"Easy, Mara. Easy. It's okay." Hallemay's arms wrapped around me as she rocked us back and forth. "You're safe. Sssh. Sssh."

"It's all right." Rochelle said.

Trembling, I opened my eyes to see her sitting at the head of the narrow bed, stroking my hair. Hallemay sat lower, holding me. The top sheet had slipped from the bed to pool on the floor, a lumpy pile of pink, leaving my blue nightgown and pale limbs exposed.

A thin band of moonlight seeped through the window, under the shade.

No Torres. Just me, Hallemay, and Rochelle.

Hallemay's skin glowed in the light. She loosened her hold on me.

My arms shook as I stretched them out in front of me. Turned them this way and that. Sat up to catch the brightest of the light and make sure upon sure they were free. Nothing bound my wrists.

The night air wasn't that cool, but more so than wherever I'd been in my dreams. I shivered and shook. Rochelle retrieved the sheet from the floor and tucked it around me. Her teeth flashed as she bent close and smiled, brushing the hair from my eyes.

"Bad dream?"

"Yeah. I'm sorry. Did I wake everyone?" The warmth from the sheet, and Hallemay still sheltering my shoulders with her arm, sank in and my shaking slowed.

"Some, maybe. You're not the first in the house to have nightmares, and you won't be the last." Rochelle and Hallemay exchanged a glance. Rochelle nodded and turned away. "I leave you in good hands. God watch you the rest of your night."

The door shut behind Rochelle with a click.

Hallemay shifted, shaking the bed as she got up and retrieved the bottle of water left on the floor. Two, in fact, mine and hers from next to the other twin bed. I took one swallow, and the water cleared the last dregs of the dream, leaving only the last taste of mint from brushing my teeth earlier. She, on the other hand, drained hers near dry.

"I'm sorry you had to . . . to hold me down. Did I hurt you?"

"No. But it's thirsty work." She sat back down next to me. "Better now?"

"Yeah."

"It's just a dream."

"Is it? Was it?"

"You're still here and still yourself."

"I dreamed of Rainbow and Spring again. Third time.

That's supposed to be the charm, right? Well it wasn't. There was an earthquake, and fires and dead people. Then ships and running, always running, trying to stay far away from Torres. Except he caught up. Somewhere . . . I was caught. Imprisoned. My wrists shackled. And then he was there, drinking from me again." Words tumbled out of me until my throat grew dry and I had to stop and drink.

Hallemay sat still beside me. Her body was straight and stiff, hands fisted and eyes closed. A single shudder ripped through her, and then she bent her head. A few tears leaked from her eyes, glittering as they trickled down her cheeks.

"You know what I dreamt, don't you?"

"It's part of the tale Grandfather hasn't told you yet." She wiped the tears away with a finger.

"Because Jesse was in the car, and then we were here, and he can't tell anyone who isn't family?"

"Yes."

"That's stupid." I punched my pillow, then laid it against the wall and moved back to lean on it.

"I understand how you'd feel that way." Hallemay didn't move.

"Yeah, right." I sniffed and kept silent for several minutes. She didn't say anything either. I broke first. "Did they get away?"

"Who?"

"Rainbow and Spring."

Her chest rose and fell as a big sigh escaped her.

"Maybe Grandfather can find some time tomorrow to—"

"No, don't make me wait. Please." Foolish to ask. I knew they hadn't escaped. They'd raised Grampa, but he wasn't born in the time I'd dreamed. All the same, the nightmare had lurched about from one horror to another, unlike the early dreams which had had a story quality to them. Then again, I had still sort of thought the whole thing was a story back then. Nevertheless, I needed to put the dream in some kind of context, time and place. "You know this as well as he."

"Not as well."

"Well enough. You can tell me the most important parts." I crossed my arms over my chest, only the movement brought back the nightmare and I dropped them back to my side. "Please?"

"I'll tell you the part you dreamed, fill in some of the details you're missing." She moved closer on the bed, her voice dropping so that I could barely hear her. "Take it or leave it, your choice."

"Tell me all you can."

Hallemay sighed again and took my hand in her cold fingers.

"After their meeting with the other spring of life on Mount Vesuvius, Rainbow and Spring made long plans to escape. They'd already convinced Torres to trust them with some knowledge and a degree of movement. Now they worked to gain the types of knowledge and resources they'd need to escape him and truly be free.

"Now understand, he could track them within a certain radius." She traced a wide circle with her free hand.

So they tracked him also and learned at just what point their sense of him verged on fading, before they turned back around. This they did several times, realizing they needed something to happen. Something to trap him while they had time to get far enough away to not know just where they had gone.

They weren't yet sure what circumstances would suffice. They weren't stupid, however, and knew they would need monies to pay for passage from wherever they were back to the Americas and on to their homeland. So they hoarded any spare coin they could find and hid them—in the hems of their clothes, a second lining in a pack—enough, they hoped, not only for passage but to keep them safe from anyone who might think to prey upon a young woman, or a woman dressed as a man, traveling alone.

As with many forced to make their own way, they learned the ways of bribes and who could be bought with coins or information.

They also picked up knowledge of languages whenever they could, the better to keep alert and safe, and learn of ports and shipping routes.

All the long while, they held distant hope they might help Torres find a magical weapon which could kill him outright. Unfortunately, although he collected weapons with a reputation for magic, they never found any which had more than a glimmer. Certainly not enough to kill someone who still regularly drank water of life from their veins.

There was one time, though Grampa is the better narrator of that tale, when they tried to work on one of Torres' competitors for magical artifacts. That turned out no better than their attempt to use the Inquisition on their behalf.

They had far more time than they wished, than anyone would wish, before the circumstances were right.

Until Torres took them east to Ragusa, in search of artifacts left by Alexander the Great.

And an earthquake hit.

Vibrations rippled through my body, a shadow of the tremors from my nightmare.

"Followed by fires, fed on winds, which raged over the city."

Flames crackled in my ears. Smoke filled my nose and mouth, until I coughed.

Rainbow and Spring managed to get a nun's habit from one of the many nunneries nearly destroyed, and wangle a place among the surviving nuns, only sixty or so out of over two hundred. They left the city the next day aboard a ship with the Archbishop Pedro de Torres, no relation to Eyague de Torres, our Torres.

Who was left behind.

And then it was a chase. Across the Adriatic. Italy. The Tyrrhenian and Alboran Seas. The Atlantic Ocean. Always trying to get far enough ahead they couldn't sense Torres behind.

They were in the clear when they finally stepped aboard an English ship bound for the Americas. For Jamaica, except . . .

Her voice broke and she turned away, arms tight against her body. Her cold fingers still clasped my hand, tighter than ever and to the point of pain. Her shoulders rose and fell as she spoke, taking long, deep breaths between words.

Someone realized they traveled alone, without protection. They never knew who betrayed them, or if they did know they did not entrust Grandfather with the information, or he me.

They were alone.

Female.

Not white.

I don't know what they taught you in school, but whites bought, sold, and worked Native Americans as slaves alongside those forcibly brought from Africa.

No sooner had Rainbow and Spring set foot on Jamaica's shores, than they were snatched and taken, despite their protests, to be sold.

They labored in the fields, not long I think, but before they could work out a way to escape, Torres caught up.

He bought them.

And carried them back to Europe, rarely letting them out of his sight.

After the remembered earthquake, I had no flashes from my nightmares or any breezes. Nothing except Torres's face.

Hallemay turned around and tried to smile, though it was little more than a shadow.

"Now, try to sleep again, and no more dreams tonight."

"No more nightmares? After that tale?" I knew it hurt her to tell me, but I couldn't keep the words in. "Why do you and Grampa always have to stop? Why won't you ever share the whole thing so I can be part of this wild chase to track Torres down?"

"You're not ready."

"Try me."

"My dear sister, you haven't let things sink in." She picked up her bottle to drink from, discovered it empty, and tossed it over to land with a soft thump on her bed.

"That's a bunch of bullshit. You're just stringing me along, but it's not like I can go anywhere except wherever you do, to Texas to find Torres anyway."

"You poor thing." She leaned back and crossed her arms. "What if I were to tell you your father shows up in the story?"

My anger and irritation vanished in an instant. I froze. Blinked two or three times.

"But . . . Grampa told him the story, too fast or whatever. How can he be in it?"

"Because of Grandfather, your father became part of the story."

"So?" My fingers started twitching, and I wove them together to keep still.

"You didn't weep, even in your dream." Hallemay ran a finger down my cheek.

"No, I don't cry. Dad always told me to keep my tears."

"He taught you well, even though he didn't have to."

A cool note entered her voice. I opened and shut my mouth a few times, but nothing came out.

"What if I told you . . ." She leaned in close enough to breathe on me, our noses almost touching. "He was wrong."

"Who?" I held my ground.

"Your father."

"About crying? It's a way of keeping power. Not showing weakness." I could hear his voice in my head.

"You didn't even give me a chance to say what he was wrong about." Hallemay shook her head. "You leapt right to defend him. You're bristling all over about his stupid ban on crying when in fact, he was wrong about a lot of things. As are we all. I accuse him of nothing more or less than can be said of me, although I prefer to think the things I am wrong about are of lesser importance than his wrongs. Nevertheless, all people have good and bad in them."

"I know. I know." I drew back, retreated until my back was against the pillow and wall. "He was a lousy boyfriend to Mom, and never there enough as a father. A holiday father Mom once called him: only around when there was fun to be had. But he did the best he could, and he always called and came for me."

"You're still leaping to his defense, but I was talking about complexities. So here's one for you to ponder." Hallemay sat back as well, head high and a cold smile curving her lips. "Through no fault or virtue of his own, he once received a gift. Something that had been stolen. When he learned this, he refused to return it to its original owner. He considered it his, and did not agree anyone else had a rightful claim."

Her words went in my ears, but . . . they didn't make sense. Dad was given a stolen gift and kept it? Not cool, but she hadn't said what the gift was. Maybe he'd spent it, or ate it or drank it. He hadn't known it was stolen, after all. She admitted as much.

At length, I finally managed to move my stiff lips and force out the question she waited for.

"Keep what?"

"Water of life."

WATER OF LIFE

Who could sleep after such an accusation?

The mattress beneath me might as well have turned to stones and rubble. The sheets seemed rough and chafed as I tossed, while residue of lavender detergent clinging to them, which I'd welcomed on first lying down, became rank to the point I wanted to pinch my nose and never stop. A sour taste bloomed in my mouth as though I'd thrown up and swallowed back down, which I hadn't.

Nothing had changed in the room—except me.

Surely Hallemay meant nothing more than Dad had got hold of some stolen water of life. Maybe water got from a spring of life with permission so that it strengthened, but nothing more.

Except, she might have said in that case.

And she hadn't. She'd shut right up after those few, hard words. Told me to sleep on things and gone back to her bed where she lay now, with her back to me.

Leaving me to stew.

Wonder.

Worry.

What if she meant Dad had done something worse?

I still believed in the dad I remembered. The man who never forgot to call when he could, found some measure of joy in every day, and cradled me in my oldest memories.

But I also liked and trusted Hallemay, or I'd never have agreed to go on this cross-country jaunt with her and Grampa. Or maybe I would've, with the dangle of wiping away those debts, but with more caution. Or something.

All I needed to sleep was some way for Hallemay and Dad both be worthy of my trust and love. Which meant she couldn't be all wrong, though she could be misled. That was the easiest assumption. Unfortunately it itched and nagged at me.

Who should I believe? What did it say about me and Dad if I accepted Hallemay's words as true? How could he still be the father I remembered?

The very direction of my thoughts sent a chill down my spine.

Because there was the fact that Dad spent his life chasing adventures without ever bringing back injuries or scars. Nor could I remember a single time he'd been sick or mentioned suffering so much as a cold.

I slipped a hand onto the bedside table and grabbed my phone. Tapped the screen three times and watched it light. My finger hovered over the button to call Mom. To have her tell me about sometime when Dad was sick, something, anything to break the cycle of fears storming through my head.

Except I didn't. Instead, I laid the phone back, face down.

A familiar memory flashed before my eyes, one I'd recalled many times since the plane crash.

Dad had come to town for a weekend, and stopped by to take me out for an afternoon. I don't remember where we went, or even if we did. Only a few, select moments of the visit lasted all the years.

Him standing at the foot of the stairs, head tilted to the side and his eyes rolling as Mom went over her usual litany of everything he was and wasn't to do with me. He wore his hair—black and fine, same as mine—long enough to brush his white collared shirt. A light sheen of sweat beaded his forehead under the warm noonday sun, and he'd taken off his blue suit jacket and slung it over one arm.

"Yes, yes, Kendra, I will take care of her. I always do."

Mom grunted, but held my hand as she walked me down the stairs. I was little, not just small and undergrown but little. Four, maybe five. She'd dressed me in sandals, dark green shorts, and a pink shirt, and tied a matching ribbon in my hair.

A gust of wind grabbed the ribbon, whipping it from my head with a sharp sting as it took hairs along. The pink strand danced before me—and I didn't want to lose it. Pulling my hand from Mom's grasp, before she realized what I meant or could tighten her fingers, I dashed after the ribbon.

I can still close my eyes and envision the serpentine twists as the wind wrapped the ribbon about itself, keeping it always ahead of me.

So caught was I that nothing else registered—not even that I'd run into the street or the squeals of the bus trying to brake.

Then a hard force grabbed me and threw me backward onto the sidewalk. I skinned my hands, not badly at all, but Mom was there an instant later. Her arms around me, tight, and her head buried in my neck.

She didn't see it all, but I did: Dad, who'd thrown me out of the way, in the middle of the street.

The bus stopping, but not in time.

Metal hitting flesh with a dull thud.

Dad's cry of pain.

His body crumpling to the ground.

Yet he lived. He lay in agony, chest rising and falling. A crowd gathered around. Mom would've kept me back, but I wriggled and pleaded, and somehow the press of people never fully blocked my view.

Because I watched him rise. Blood and dirt from the street stained his shirt, with some still streaming from his nose. He clapped a hand over it. Wincing, he limped over to crumple next to me and grab me tighter than Mom, if that was possible. He refused to go to the hospital, though he accepted some pain pills. The next day he complained some about being sore, but otherwise showed no signs of injuries.

I would have sworn he hadn't bled much—that the stains on his shirt were mostly dirt from the street.

This time, though, as the scene flashed before me, the amount of blood registered. Much more than I'd thought. On his back, as much as his front, where the bloody nose couldn't be to blame.

He'd been injured—and healed fast.

Really fast.

What if he did drink the water of life, the kind that gave youth and health . . . but worse, how could he have gotten hold of it? He'd have to have tracked a spring down.

No way, no how, would he have found Torres and drunk from Rainbow.

RIDDLES

"*A*re you awake?"

Well, I wasn't but the high-pitched whisper changed things. I kept my eyes closed, the better to enjoy the last bits of slumber. The pillow was so soft, the bed too. Besides, raising my eyelids would take energy. My eyes, my whole face, felt gritty as though dusted with sand. Sun beat down on me, warming my body and making me see only red.

No, not only red. A thin breeze wound around my head, flashing a vision of baby alligators sunning themselves on rocks in the middle of a pool of water. They had to curl up to make the most of the sunlight, for it sifted in thin streams through tall trees and thick, leafy branches.

Then savory scents floated through the air—biscuits, bacon, coffee. My mouth watered and a rumble escaped my stomach.

The bed lurched and rocked. The sheet over me slipped off, and the breeze stopped feeding me the vision in favor of rustling over my skin until nearly every hair I had stood stock straight.

Warm breath redolent of bacon and gravy exhaled near my ear.

"You are awake! I knew it! Time for breakfast."

I let myself be bullied and chivvied into getting dressed in my usual attire, jeans and shirt and shoes and socks. Packed up my bag, and then sat on the bed while Rayla combed my hair. She had wonderful soft hands, smoothing the strands after every stroke. Made me sniff, remembering when I was little and Mom used to take the time to do more than a pony tail or single braid. Rayla tried various twists, her breath huffing as she complained about how fly-away it was. In the end, she turned it into four thin braids, two on either side.

She took my hand and walked me downstairs to the kitchen. It was almost empty, although given the number of dirty dishes on the table it hadn't been only a little while ago.

Rochelle turned from the sink and gave me a broad smile. A moment later, she had me sat down at the table with a full plate of biscuits, bacon, and gravy. She also sent Rayla off to find her brother once it was clear the girl wanted to feed me as though I were a doll.

Only three people remained in the kitchen. Rochelle clearing the table, me eating, and Grampa nodding over a mug of coffee. His head hung low after one glance my way. The lines on his face seemed to have deepened, and his eyes were almost as saggy as mine must be. He'd rolled his orange shirt sleeves half way up his forearms and left the top two buttons undone.

"Hallemay told me she talked to you last night some," he said, low but audible over the clatter of dishes piling next to the sink. "She spoke out of turn."

"You mean she was wrong?" My breath caught in my throat, so I barely got the words out.

He shook his head, not looking at me.

"It wasn't the time or place. We're not at the right point in the story."

"You're saying Dad did drink stolen water of life?" My fork tines chimed against the plate and I set it down, the last bite of bacon turning rancid in my mouth. "From where? Rainbow?"

"Your father never drank from Rainbow." His whole body gave one big shake.

A rill of relief rippled from head to knees, then stopped. He hadn't said a whole no.

"But he did drink stolen water of life?" I asked, hoping for a no.

"It's complicated."

That line again?

"So tell me!"

"When we get to that part of the story."

"Do you have any idea what you're putting me through?"

"I've risked too much to get to this point, and you are too precious to me to rush things." He lifted his head and caressed my cheek for a moment. "I know I am asking a lot of you but trust me, just this much."

"What do you want me to do, hate Dad?" Now I was the one with my head hanging low, staring at my plate.

"Never." Another caress of my cheek. "He was my son, my firstborn, and I love him still. I disagreed with him on certain important points, but I never stopped loving him. Believe that, Mara. I don't ask you to hate him. He did what he thought was right by his lights. I am taking the long road— and you can hate me for that in the end, if you like, though I hope you will understand—because when we come to the end I hope you will see things the way I do, not the way he did. All because I told him too fast."

The chair scraped against the tiled floor as he shoved it

back. He stroked my back as he left with a soft word to Rochelle.

My head was too thick for me to think fast, or I'd have been hot on his heels. Instead, I'd barely started to push my chair back when Rochelle dropped into Grampa's vacated chair and laid a warm, damp hand on mine.

"Easy, now. Some things are better let sit a while." She nodded in the direction he'd gone. "And you look to need another night or two in bed. Did you sleep at all?"

"Some. A little." I shrugged. "It wasn't any problem with the bed or anything, just . . ."

"I've known Hallemay as long I knew anybody, and she's always tackled the hard road straight on. So long as you ride with her, that'll be your road, too."

Just what I didn't want to hear. I studied Rochelle, watching her watching me. The notion of asking her about Torres tempted me, but not for long. No guarantee she knew it, not with Grampa and Hallemay saying it was only for family. Instead I asked a different question.

"Did you ever meet my father? Robert de Leon. Er, Carlos."

Nothing for a long moment except a look of puzzlement. Then a flicker of something in her eyes. She leaned back and studied me. Her mouth opened and shut a few times before she shook her head.

"No."

I had no way of knowing if it was a truth or a lie. The next moment, though, she leaned forward and took my hands in hers.

"I tell you this, though. No matter what Hallemay ever asks of you, it's nothing she wouldn't ask of herself."

Great. More cryptic utterances. I should know better than to ask, except all these mysteries kept eating away at me.

"Okay." I shrugged.

She pressed my hands and didn't release them.

"I have a message for you from Mayanna. A repeat request."

"Okay." I settled back, though I might've pushed my plate away. I couldn't eat anything anymore.

"Hallemay's with her now. Mayanna understands her mother has to go, but asks you to comfort her if she needs it. Remind her Mayanna loves Grandmother, too."

It was the same message I'd carried yesterday, except . . . now I thought about it, had Mayanna said Grandmother or Grandfather? I'd thought I'd misheard, but maybe she'd said mother. Back when we first left Philly, all of three days ago, I'd have sworn Grampa wasn't married. I hadn't met every relative on my father's side, Grampa admitted that straight out, but I'd have thought he'd have told me if he was married. Or maybe even brought his wife with him.

Now, I couldn't say near anything for sure and certain. Not even who to trust.

Not Rochelle.

Not Hallemay.

Not Grampa.

I had no reason one way or the other to trust Jesse, either, but a little later I found myself alone with him. He wore a lightweight tunic, the fringe dancing against his jean-clad legs. Light brown leather shoes shuffled against the ground as we loaded the car.

So much easier now the tank collapsed even further. Shouldn't take long, pretty much just slinging in one bag after another except for Hallemay's camera bags which we put safe on one side. Except one of the bags stuck on something at the back and wouldn't lay flat. We wound up unloading and shuffling things but they still didn't fit, so we took them out again.

I scrambled half in, being smaller and lighter, and pushed the bags aside to find the hold-up.

Two dark things, blending into the smooth fabric covering the wayback, stretched nearly the whole width of the car. One proved to be a hard-sided, rectangular case which had caught on the other object so that neither lay flat. At the end opposite the tank, the second object ended in a cross-like part half dull gray and half dark and topped with a circle.

Only when I put my hand on it did I realize Grampa really had a sword in the car. I picked it up expecting something heavy but it wasn't. So I went reeling back and nearly tumbled out of the car as I pulled and the sword came free of the scabbard, the end having caught under the hard-sided case. Jesse braced me. He took the sword laid it lengthwise on the car bed, then worked the scabbard free.

The scabbard blended well with the fabric lining the car, dark leather with a few scratches and creases here and there. Nearly a meter long, they appeared heavier than they were. Leather matching the scabbard wrapped around the hilt, except for the circular piece. It didn't seem fancy at all to me, no gilding or precious metals: just a long, sharp weapon meant for killing. The sharpness, at least, I could attest to, for I ran a finger across the width and got my skin sliced. Just a small cut, which healed fast enough.

All the same, a series of shivers ran down my spine. I don't think I'd ever had so many, even in the depth of winter, as in traveling with Grampa and Hallemay.

Without a word, Jesse sheathed the sword and angled it across the wayback. He piled our bags atop it, nearly burying it from sight.

That was the moment I risked opening my mouth and asking him why he'd decided to apprentice to Hallemay.

He halted with one hand braced on the car frame and

turned, dark eyes fixing on me. The usual easy curve to his smile flattened into a line.

"That's a very personal question."

I looked away first.

"My reasons are my own," he said. "I will share one. After riding with a number of pathwalkers and wayfinders, I feel Hallemay offers the clearest and most understandable explanations of why she takes the turns she does."

The code-speak I'd heard between them didn't sound like explanations to me. More impressions of what they saw when they considered different turns. Maybe they talked more other times, outside the car, or when I wasn't around. I didn't dare ask how long it took to get explanations from Hallemay. Shorter than for me, no doubt.

Maybe, just maybe, she or Grampa would finally get to the end and I'd understand.

BAYOU ALLIGATORS

That afternoon, I slipped back into the car and slumped into my usual seat. The soft cover was warm, since the car had sat in full sun while we ate lunch and managed not to talk to each other much. The padding beneath me had started to conform to my shape. I wound up planting my bottom in exactly the same spot, because sitting anyway else wasn't comfy for long. At least it didn't creak beneath me. Grampa settled into the front seat and made up for that with his shifting and rattling.

Then Hallemay slid into the backseat next to me, and I startled in surprise.

Because she didn't do the backseat. Not ever. It was her car, and the driver's seat belonged to her. The only person she let drive was Jesse, and him in short stretches while she sat in the front passenger and quizzed him on anything she cared to ask about. Maybe she didn't trust us to go the right way if she wasn't up front. Or didn't like the backseat, for which I wouldn't blame her as it wasn't particularly comfortable.

Yet here she was, folding her long legs into the narrow

space—but angled, so she could lean against the side easy, even with the seat belt buckled.

Jesse settled into the front and cast an inquiring glance back at her.

"Head for Houston by whatever road seems best to you." Shoulders hunched, she yawned.

"Anything else?"

"No, just that." She yawned again. "Give me an hour or two of rest and we can work through the route and alternate choices."

"Rest well."

For a moment, the angle of the rearview mirror reflected a slice of his face—wide eyes and an incredulous smile. Then he adjusted it, and I lost the view. A low thrum vibrated through the car as he started the motor and headed off.

Grampa grunted and settled back in his seat, leaning his head against the side of the car just like Hallemay.

Within minutes, they both started snoring.

Leaving me to wallow in my seat, going round and round the same ideas about Dad getting stolen water of life but at least not drinking from Rainbow's blood. And Torres being in West Texas and Grampa knowing but not saying.

Plus the same stew of mulling over Grampa and Hallemay keeping secrets as I'd been doing for days now.

Without any new insights, or ideas about how to escape the endless cycle short of hiking my way back home, which wasn't really an option. I owed Grampa.

And no matter what, I had to know how the story ended.

I didn't pay any attention to where we were going, because what did I know? Hallemay didn't even keep any maps around that I'd seen.

So between me not knowing and Hallemay and Grampa sleeping and Jesse choosing the way, he took a wrong turn.

Or two, or five, or maybe just one compounded by not turning around.

No way could I not notice, because eventually he turned down a narrow dirt road. Ill-kept, it had little more than two tracks for tires. The car jounced up and down at uneven pitches.

Trees grew up close on either side, their thick roots helping hold the dirt in place—I hoped. Light flashed now and then between them as the sun reflected off still waters. Hot and muggy air seeped through the open windows carrying a dank, marsh smell so heavy it coated my tongue to the point I couldn't taste anything else.

The track didn't go far before it dead-ended in a small clearing with just enough room for a small car—which this wasn't—to turn around.

Jesse pulled as far as he could to one side and turned off the motor. His hands clung to the wheel, but his arms were shaking hard enough no one could miss.

I didn't know what any of the trees or plants or insects or birds were around us—but it looked picture perfect for any glossy magazine about visiting Louisiana. Immense trees, bigger than those lining the track, rose from roots planted in the slow-moving water which surrounded the clearing. Sticks and leaves lay scattered on the ground, except beneath the faint tracks of previous cars stopping and parking. Moss-draped branches, offering a myriad of hiding places for birds. Bits of plumage—white, blue, purple—flashed here and there on occasion, sometimes easily visible and others half-hidden by the layer of pollen filling the air.

Both Grampa and Hallemay had roused, matching confusion on their faces as they gazed around the clearing.

"In what world is this Houston?" Grampa got his dig in first. He opened his door and stepped out. Holding onto the frame, he stretched and his back crackled.

"We're where we're supposed to be." Jesse followed suit, but with less cracking and more holding so tight to the car the blood drained from his knuckles. "Why it's here, I don't . . ."

Hallemay pushed the driver's seat forward and got out. Rather than stretching, she marched around the clearing in a circle ending right in front of Jesse. Hands on her hips, she gave a sigh.

"Well, that's a lesson on me for not waking more often to pay attention. Let's work it back and figure out where you went astray, then we can get back on the road."

"Nothing seemed wrong." Jesse shook his head.

"Then why are we here?"

Off they went, back to phrases I hadn't a chance of understanding. A thin layer of pollen had started accumulating on the top of the car. They took turns drawing maps in it.

If everyone else had got out enough to stretch their legs, I didn't see any point in staying inside.

The humidity hit even stronger out of the car. The marsh smell still coated my tongue, but otherwise my skin sure liked the silky feel of the air. Not so much the whine of mosquitoes, but there were some around. I grabbed my water bottle and took a swig, hoping maybe it'd make me less interesting to bugs.

A low bellow rang out right next to me.

I jumped, nearly dropping the bottle as my fingers tightened. Then I looked down, and jumped again.

A small alligator, at most a third of a meter, sat right next to my foot.

Somehow it had waddled over to me without my noticing. No matter how much it blended in with the mix of leaves and earth, I should've noticed. Grayish, bony plates covered the back except for bright yellow stripes on the flat tail. The small size didn't make the long, rounded snout look that much smaller—or the teeth any less sharp.

It wasn't bellowing at me, though, but the two more who followed behind.

They hissed and gave their own bellows in return. Then they seemed to come to some accord, because the one closest to me started a bellow, only to turn it into that odd sound Grampa made, purr-chompf. Only softer and higher.

All three made an awkward triangle around me. Their snouts pressed close enough to scrape my ankles.

I barely breathed, holding as still as I could. Impersonating a tree—only my knees knocked, hands shook, and teeth chattered because who cared if they were baby alligators they were still *alligators* and there were three of them to one of me, not counting all their teeth.

Plus, if there were baby alligators around, might there be a mama alligator near, too? I'd read about female alligators caring for their young on at least one or another of the many recent visits to zoos.

"Easy, now, Mara, stay where you are." Grampa gave a purr-chompf, which the babies ignored except for one lashing its tail. "They just want to smell you."

"Oh, is that all?"

Taking deep breaths required a lot of concentration. In for a count of six, out to a count of twelve. It helped. My knees stopped knocking and teeth chattering, though my fingers kept shaking.

Jesse knelt and picked up a thick stick from the ground. He thumped the end against the earth, raising a hollow thud.

All three alligators stopped for a moment to hiss before flicking their tails at him and going back to sniffing my ankles and feet.

A much deeper bellow and grunt sent the babies scattering, tails flicking. They might not be fast, but that didn't mean they moved slow. In a few moments, they slipped into the water.

A much, much bigger alligator, no doubt mama, emerged from the water nearby. Dark lines marked her tail, but otherwise she was longer version of the babies—nearly three meters. She waddled over to Grampa. I let out a shuddering breath as he stood tall.

The alligator gave another loud, deep bellow.

Jesse moved towards Grampa.

"Hold." Grampa said to him, raising a hand palm out.

Opening his mouth wide and curving his chest, he gave a warm, vibrant purr-chompf.

All he got in return was a good view of sharp teeth—visible even several meters away from where I stood—and a third bellow.

The breezes weren't much help. I had no warning about the baby gators, nor did the breezes translate any of their noises.

As for the bigger, a breeze did blow a few stray sensations my way. The splashing of the hunt and capture. Teeth gnashing and rending flesh. The pitiful cries of baby alligators as they were caught, killed, and eaten. The scrape of teeth brushing my skin so real I had to run my hands over my belly to make sure I wasn't getting bit.

With a last grunt, she turned around and lashed her tail at Grampa. She didn't hit him, but came close.

Then set off towards me.

"She won't hurt you. Just keep still." Grampa sagged back against a tree trunk. Hallemay braced him on one side.

Jesse paced the gator, holding the stick ready. It looked thick and heavy in his hands. Enough to outlast a snout of sharp teeth? Maybe not.

I trembled from the effort to not move.

The alligator shambled close enough to touch me with

the end of her snout, except she didn't. Instead, she slowly opened her mouth wide and gave me a really good look down that pink gullet.

Her snout snapped together, fast as a snap of fingers.

I started, shifting several centimeters backwards and grabbing at the car to keep from falling.

She gave a satisfied nod, and that wasn't just me anthropomorphizing, then waddled back over to slip into the water.

Jesse dropped the stick, which hit the ground with a clunk, and grabbed hold of me. His warm hands opened the door and tucked me into the car. He slipped into the backseat next to me, fastening my seatbelt when I kept trembling, and then warming my cold fingers between his.

Hallemay followed with Grampa a moment later. He managed to fasten his own seat belt. She did a three-point turn and headed back down the track. No one said a word until she gave a heavy sigh and broke the silence.

"Well, that was too interesting to be a completely wrong turn. Jesse, I apologize for saying you went astray."

Jesse didn't get a chance to respond.

"I didn't think things would go bad for the alligators." Grampa slumped in his seat, head in his hands. "I could've ended this ages ago if I'd only . . ."

"You had other priorities." Hallemay kept her hands on the wheel, but shrugged her shoulders.

"That doesn't excuse it. I didn't think." Grampa shook his head and straightened, slapping his hands against his thighs. "Well, it ends now. This time we catch and kill Torres."

SECRETS

Something something something. Strange words I didn't recognize over and over.

A good meal filled my stomach. The taste of spiced rice and beans lingered in my mouth. An easy breeze kept the warm, humid air moving. Hallemay lay back on the sofa, one hand over her eyes and her legs dangling from the knee down. One shoe had fallen, a simple blue slip-on against the red-on-gold carpeting. The other still hooked over her toes.

Jesse stood by a wide triple window, looking out. The sun had started to descend towards the horizon, its rays gaining a similar gold tone and gilding him where he stood with the pale yellow curtains swaying behind him.

For my part, my body sank into a soft chair very different from the car seat. The cushion adapted itself to my body, although it was a little tall for me so my feet barely brushed the ground. The gold fabric didn't hold heat, so it retained a hint of coolness despite the general warmth. Definitely nicer than anything I'd sat in back home. Grampa'd gotten an unexpected upgrade for us into a two-bedroom suite, with this common area.

Which meant I could leave and retreat into the bedroom I'd share with Hallemay, and not have to hear him.

Something something Mara something. Grampa kept talking, swinging the cord with one hand as he paced back and forth.

Now and then a name I recognized: Jesse, Hallemay . . . my name.

Except I had no idea what language Grampa spoke. That in and of itself was nothing new. There were a lot of languages floating around. Every couple of years when I was still in school, we'd have a language basics unit covering some of the different languages spoken in the nation. By law, all public schools had to teach students at least one European language, preferably English, Spanish, or French, and at least one Indigenous language. My school in Philly taught all students English and Lenape, with additional languages being an option but you had to pay. I learned Spanish for a couple of years when Mom had the money, and then not.

Unfortunately, all that meant was I could figure out what Grampa wasn't speaking, not what he was. Not English, not Spanish, not Lenape, and certainly not any of the Algonquian languages related to Lenape. Nor did it resemble any other language groups I remembered being exposed to in school, i.e. not Na-Dené or Algic or Uto-Aztecan.

Whatever it was, Jesse didn't seem to comprehend, so it wasn't a variant of his language. Hallemay did follow along for she let drop a phrase now and then, although her speaking knowledge was halting and much slower than Grampa's command. Sometimes he nodded and repeated what she'd said, other times not.

But I couldn't ask her. Well, I could except she didn't seem too approachable, not since we'd left NOGA and her daughter, and I didn't want to stress her any more than I had to.

My legs twitched, feet tapping against the chair legs and toes brushing against the ground.

Grampa glanced my way, and his lips tightened.

Hallemay sighed and shook her head.

I got up, stretching to the point the bones in my neck cracked. This earned me another sigh.

Whiffs of wildflowers, sweet and tart, lured me to the window. The trim green lawn stretched only a few feet beyond the hotel. Elsewise, wildflowers tipped in purples, reds, and blues filled the vista. A path twisted through them, winding down towards something that gleamed in the setting sun.

A river.

The sun hung far enough above the horizon we should have time to meander down to the river and back.

"I'm going for a walk." I kept my voice low, so as not to disturb Grampa or keep him from hearing the tinny voice on the other end of his call. "Anyone want to join me?"

Hallemay and Jesse exchanged looks. They didn't say anything, but Jesse stepped up beside me with the alacrity of someone who'd been volunteered.

It took longer than I thought to make our way out of the hotel. Hallemay had wrinkled her nose at staying here, but her favorite place to stop had suffered a fire since her last pass-thru, and this was the nearest acceptable place with vacancies. My feet sank into the thick carpet with every step. Both Jesse's and my shoe soles made a shushing noise as we walked.

Neither of us talked.

Me, because most of the things I wanted to talk about, Jesse didn't know anything about. Namely the never-ending story of Rainbow, Spring, and Torres. As for any anything I'd ask about him, it might count as a personal questions and I didn't want to intrude again.

Why he didn't talk, I couldn't guess. Though I regularly wondered what went through his head about all of us, that fell in the category of one of the questions I wouldn't ask.

Then he bent and sniffed a big shrub with pale yellow, star-shaped flowers near which bees hovered and hummed.

"What is it?" At last, a safe question to ask. The petals had a fruity smell. I didn't recognize them, or expect to.

"I don't know." He shook his head.

Neither of us proved to have any idea what most of the flowers were, but it got us talking some of the time at least. The flowers might've listened in, if they knew English, for some of the plants swapped places as we passed.

There hadn't been much sign of land movement at our last stops, other than the bayou with the alligators, but here the gravel path had several dips. A few small sink-holes nibbled at the edges here and there. In at least two places, thick roots made for uneven ridges in the path.

I didn't care. Every breath brought in more sweet scents. The river burbled gently when we reached it, glittering in the last rays of sunlight passing through the trees on the far side. A couple of those I recognized: magnolias, crepe myrtles, but nothing else.

"No alligators in sight." Jesse chuckled after checking the water.

"Good." I gave a sigh, sounding like Hallemay to my own ears. "I've seen enough to last a lifetime."

We stayed later than we should have, letting the quiet beauty wash over us. By the time we turned to go, the light had started to vanish except in the distance where the hotel gave off a warm glow.

The ground rippled. Something burrowing through or another shift. A small sinkhole appeared beneath my feet—I saw it too late. My step went wrong and I fell.

My hands and knees hit the earth at the same moment.

Pain lanced through me, and I gave a cry. Jesse hissed only a moment later as he, too, dropped with a thud.

I rolled to the side and sat, rocking as the first flash of pain settled into a dull thud. Drops of blood covered my hands. The gravel must've been fresh, for it was sharp. A few pieces lodged in my skin. I flicked them away, wincing as each left a bloody pock-mark behind. My knees ached, but my jeans had protected my skin.

Jesse likewise had bloodied hands and no marks on his jeans. He rolled to the side then jumped to his feet without setting a hand against the ground—something I couldn't do —and oh I wished for that strength and agility.

Before I could push myself up, he offered the less-injured of his hands, bearing only one long scrape across the middle and a few spots of blood at the base. I hooked my fingers over his and let him give me a pull.

A moment later he hissed again, this time over the state of my palms. With a whistling sound, he pulled a handkerchief from his pocket and dabbed at my wounds. A few drops of blood stained the checkered red and white cloth, but my hand had already started to scab.

"Don't bother." I pulled away, gently. "I heal fast. Take care of yourself."

"We both need to wash our hands." He hustled back to the hotel, but not so fast I couldn't keep up.

Into the hotel, up the stairs, and along the hall all in a few long strides which left me gasping for air. Then we stopped at the door.

I reached for the handle.

Jesse got there first—except his hand closed not over the metal knob but my wrist.

He turned my hand over and stared.

Pink skin mottled with a few red lines and marks shone under the yellowish hall light. The scrapes had closed, as usual. Indeed, with every passing moment the wounds became harder to see.

"I told you I heal fast."

"No." He shook his head, earrings catching the light and bouncing beams around. "I heal fast."

He held his palm out next to mine, the same hand he'd offered me earlier. The blood drops on the base of his hand had turned dark red and started to scab. So had most of the long scrape, except for a drop at one end and another in the middle.

We'd been hurt about the same. Yet as we watched, some of the marks on my palms vanished.

"I've never seen anyone heal so quick. It must be magic." Dark brown eyes fixed on me, lines forming on his brow. "Who, or what, are you?"

My mouth hung open. I shrank back from his gaze, shoulders rising close to my ears.

"I'm just me."

He shook his head, but before he could say anything else the door opened. Grampa glanced at both of us, then turned to Jesse and set his hands together.

"I have permission to share our family's story with you."

FRONT SEAT

For the first time, I sat in the front.

The car seat dwarfed me. The headrest loomed over me, the back seemed to curve around my shoulders, and I had far too much space for my feet. Every movement, no matter how slight, set the springs squeaking. The noise jangled in my ears.

Worse, the road stretched out straight in front of me, lined with trees although fewer than earlier in the day. The direct line of view messed with my perceptions. No matter that I knew cars headed the other way kept to their own lanes, my body stiffened every time a car drew near. Muscles ached from shoulders to fingers and toes. The sun beat down through the windshield, warming me but not enough to compensate.

I hadn't realized until now that Hallemay hummed. She stopped on occasion, usually when we reached an intersection, but once in the middle of a fortunately empty road to ask Jesse's opinion on which way to go—though less frequently today than before. Otherwise she generated a tuneless rumbling, inaudible to the backseat but quite clear in the front, that resonated with the low thrum of the motor to vibrate in my ears and teeth.

Still, I focused on her hum in preference to the murmur of voices in the back. When I concentrated, the words came through clear as bells. I listened in at the start, but stopped soon after.

Not because I knew what Grampa said, although he was sharing the story of Rainbow and Spring with Jesse so I had a fair idea, but because I kept getting flashes. Maybe the work of the little breeze dancing within the car, but maybe not.

When I listened, ghostly echoes of the story scraped along my skin or whispered in my ears.

When I didn't, nothing.

Easy choice.

Grampa told the story in installments with breaks between, letting Jesse and Hallemay do their pathwalker code-talking—but he didn't break as long as with me. He expected to catch Jesse up to where he'd got me by late afternoon.

Then what?

Did I really want to know the answer? The butter on the egg toast I'd eaten for breakfast lingered in my mouth, about the only thing sweet remaining.

Turning my hands over, I stroked my fingers across each clear, unmarked palm in turn.

I healed fast, but surely Jesse exaggerated when he called it magic.

No. Not me. I'd been tested, for heaven's sake. Anyone enrolled with the Philly schools was tested at entry, fourth grade, and eighth grade.

I only remembered being told I didn't have any of the main magics—calling or shaping or finding or unbinding. Nor did I have any of the minor magics which people didn't talk about so much, but neither had anyone ever mentioned any magic involving healing.

Then again, none of the tests for magic involved blood or any other bodily fluid.

I was just a healthy person, maybe healthier than most, but that was it.

Nothing else.

Not different.

Except, little flickers of memories that had never bothered me before kept licking me as though I sat in the middle of a fire insisting I didn't see flames.

Mom and Louis both always got at least one cold every winter.

Not me.

I didn't have to call Mom to ask about that—or risk having her wonder why I asked.

Colds and other infectious diseases—flu and noro and who knew how many other viruses—ripped through school every year. Most of my schoolmates stayed home sick at least a couple times each year.

I'd never missed a day.

Dad saved me from the bus that time, so he'd worried it could kill me.

But he'd never been sick a day in his life either. It took an airplane crash to take him down.

What made him different—or me?

Hallemay said he'd received a gift of stolen water of life which he didn't give back.

Not cool, not right. Giving was serious business. Even between family members, anything other than an equal exchange left someone up and someone down. The best gifting practice was never to accept anything one couldn't return in equitable measure.

What could Dad have done to warrant a gift of water of life?

Stolen water of life.

Dad didn't steal it, so Hallemay said. That meant he didn't deserve to suffer for the thief's sins. Neither did the original owner—a spring of life—and it belonged to the spring rightfully, not him. He should have given it back.

What if he'd already drunk it? He'd have no way to return it, though he could at least apologize.

Except, drinking the water shouldn't have done anything for him. Grampa said that, at a distance the water only gave strength, and even that was conditional on the spring's consent. In which case it wasn't stolen.

Besides, if Dad drank it, that wouldn't have done anything for me.

Unless he drank it before I was born, or even conceived, and somehow passed it to me that way? I shivered and shied away from that line of thought because it meant thinking about my parents together that way. . . no, just no.

He hadn't drunk from Rainbow's veins, at least.

Unless someone else learned from Torres how to steal a spring, and Grampa and Hallemay split hairs when they said Dad hadn't drunk from Rainbow because he'd drunk from someone else?

No, Dad wouldn't do that.

And even if he had, he wouldn't make me drink blood, which I hadn't ever, so it didn't explain why I stayed healthy and healed fast.

I kept going in circles until my head ached.

Because other things tormented me alongside the whole matter of how and why Dad and I healed fast. The dreams I'd had of Rainbow and Spring, and the visceral experiences when Grampa told the story . . . where did they come from?

I didn't have a spring of life in my head or body. All the same, everything led back to Jesse's question.

What was I?

Not something I could ask Mom on our nightly calls, which were becoming ever shorter. Nothing more than check-ins to see we all were okay. Because what could I say? Philly and home seemed so far away.

I dreamed again last night, but not as before. Not whole visions reliving someone else's past but fragments.

First, layers of cloth wrapped around me, pinning my legs together and my arms by my side. I was curved over a shoulder. A firm hand patted my back. I burped, and a thin stream of milky white trickled out of my mouth. A soft voice whispered words I didn't understand. Warm hands eased me into the comforting cradle of two beloved arms. My mother held me close—except when I stared up at her I didn't see *my* mom.

Then I lay flat on a hard surface. Darkness filled the chamber, except where a blazing fire burned on a stone hearth. My whole body stretched taut, hands bound over my head and ankles tied together. A heavy weight pressed on my chest and belly so I couldn't even wriggle side to side. The edges dug in, hurting me. I cried, then a hand clapped over my mouth. Torres's hated face loomed over me. A blade flashed orange in the light as he cut open my neck and bent to drank. His tongue flicked against the edges of the wound, then he drew back with a grimace.

The dream changed to a ship's deck. A briny scent filled the air, along with the stench of too many unwashed bodies in too small a place. I stood crammed among a cluster of quarreling men. High above me, on another deck, two women stood near the bow of the ship. A brisk wind tangled their skirts together, mixing brown and blue, then they separated. The woman in blue turned and scanned the crowd among whom I stood. Her eyes met mine for a long moment and I recognized the woman from the first dream fragment, my mother who wasn't Mom. A moment later, she climbed the railing and leapt into the sea.

Last of all, an enormous alligator clambered out of a muddy riverbank. Sharp, white teeth flashed against the dull gray and green scales. His tail thrashing, he lashed out at my legs.

At which point I'd woken, muddled and shivering, sure and certain something was missing.

No matter how much I dreaded it, I had to know the end of the story.

RAINBOW'S CHILD

*H*allemay stopped that evening for dinner at an L-shaped building atop a hill with a long veranda offering views of Texas hills. They stretched out before us, separated by dips and shadowed valleys as the flat peaks lit with a golden haze under the setting sun. She had favored places to eat everywhere under the sun, usually featuring spicy food involving beans and rice or tortillas. Savory scents of beef and barbecue sauce cooking over a hot grill had my stomach rumbling.

Blue-and-white striped cloth covered our table at the far end of the veranda. Floor boards squeaked beneath our feet. The heat of the day had started to subside, though sweat still beaded my forehead and kept my thin shirt sticking to the small of my back after hours in the car.

The menu chalked on a board proclaimed the food too good not to eat with fingers. A passing waiter smiled as he dropped off shallow bowls of water to clean our hands. Another brought water to drink and took our orders for barbecue all-round. Alike enough to be brothers, and maybe they were. Both had round faces, long limbs, and deft hands.

They welcomed Hallemay and Grampa in Spanish accompanied with handshakes and heads shaken over how long it'd been since they'd seen them.

Then they left us alone.

Grampa gave a measured glance at the distance separating our table from other diners. Soft words and phrases floated in the air, but I'd have to concentrate to know what anyone said. All the same, he lifted a finger in the air. A breeze whipped around it, then settled into a soft whirl around us that muffled the others' voices.

"Both of you have now heard how Rainbow and Spring escaped to Jamaica, before recapture."

I nodded, leaning forward against the table.

Jesse had his arms crossed over his chest. A muscle in his cheek twitched, then he nodded as well.

What you must remember is that Torres did not trust Rainbow or Spring. They knew this. Yet they had hope, for they saw how Torres aged over the months they spent apart. His black hair became streaked with gray, and wrinkles wreathed his face.

And more, they had tasted freedom—walking apart from his shadow, breathing air untainted by his presence, standing at the bow of a ship gazing westward toward their homes.

They were no longer willing to play the game as they did before, becoming subservient and seemingly trustworthy all the while waiting for an opportunity to strike and flee.

This time, they devised a plan that allowed them to act.

They didn't recognize the flaws until far too late.

Grampa's voice grew thin and his throat tight. His hands shook. He flexed them, massaging the fingers in one and then the other. Reaching for his glass of water, he drained it in one go. His mouth and nose lifted in a grimace before settling back into their usual lines.

With a gentle tug, Jesse removed the glass from Grampa's hand and rose. The boards squeaked and the breeze made a sucking sound as he left the table. His legs moved fast and he soon vanished into the main body of the restaurant.

Grampa closed his eyes and rested his head on his entwined fingers.

Hallemay hadn't said much of anything since we stopped. Her eyes looked tired, her lids drooping, but she kept rapping her fingers at first against the table. That made too much noise so she shifted to her thigh. Every time her arm moved or leg jiggled some of the vibrations extended to me.

Worse, she stared at me. Not just a casual look considering she twisted in her seat to see me properly. She watched, studied, analyzed my every move, every breath to the point my legs started twitching and I wove my fingers together in my lap to keep from tapping too.

"Are you okay?" I asked, leaning over and keeping my voice low. "You seem tired."

"Just old memories haunting me. Sometimes when you do the right thing, it comes around and bites you in the . . ." She shrugged, then shook her head. "This will pass."

And that was that.

A minute or two later, Jesse came back with the glass filled to the brim. Somehow he managed to walk fast without spilling a drop, making me watch his careful steps with envy.

When he placed the glass in front of Grampa, the faint scent of water of life filled the air.

Grampa nodded in thanks, which Jesse accepted with a shrug of his shoulder as he reseated himself.

A lump formed in my stomach because I wasn't the one who'd gone to help. Didn't even think of it.

Then again, I wasn't ever sure, not quite, whether Grampa found telling the tale hard, or played it up to keep me strung tight as he fed me the story bit by bit. Or both, for that matter.

Jesse had it easy. He'd gotten in one big gulp what Grampa and Hallemay took days to dribble to me.

Grampa sipped from the glass. A thin layer of sweat covered his forehead. He wrapped a hand around the head of the cane he was using again, for the first time since we left Georgia.

"So, what was the plan? The flaws?" I drank from the glass in front of me. The water tasted flat, compared to the water of life, but I wasn't running out to grab more for myself. Not now. Not on the brink of moving further.

"They worked backwards. First, they started with their goal: freedom, in the places where they belonged. All of their earlier attempts had involved dealing with Torres in Europe—first killing him and then, when they could not accomplish that, escape." Grampa took another sip. "This time, instead, they plotted to take him with them. Rainbow's family were dead by then. She knew that, mourned them as the decades passed, but her people remained. Though she had met none in her travels, she had encountered others brought across the seas from lands near hers. Some, even, who spoke one of the trade tongues she learned as a child, if not her native language. These and others had tried to help her get free."

"They did?" I reared back so hard my chair rocked for a moment.

"Of course." Grampa shook his head at me. "Why would you think they would not?"

"Because you never mentioned it?"

"I told you Rainbow and Spring tried various means to escape. That they had help on occasion, but most who helped them died."

"Yeah, but that's all you said. Nothing more, no details or anything." Glancing to either side, neither Hallemay nor Jesse seemed surprised. I hadn't listened, much, as Grampa recounted it to Jesse earlier, but maybe he'd gotten a different version.

"I thought you wanted to get to the end of the story. To tell you in detail of every attempt Rainbow and Spring made to escape would slow everything down." Grampa wagged a finger at me. "Is that what you want?"

"No."

"Just as well," he nodded, his voice gentling. "The stories of those who tried to help Rainbow and Spring are not wholly mine to share. Those who survived lived to tell their tales. Those who didn't, well, their peoples know what happened, where I could find them. I took care of that when I had the chance."

"You took word?" Jesse asked.

"Word and more." Grampa's lips tightened. "Torres kept . . . souvenirs. I returned those."

"Enough." Hallemay said, touching my hand briefly. "Let Grandfather tell this his way. There will be time enough for questions later."

Jesse seemed satisfied. I wasn't so content.

For as soon as Grampa first mentioned people trying to help Rainbow and Spring, faces began to flash before my face. Women and men. Old and young. Brown and white. A surge of tenderness rose within me—though the feeling didn't belong to me—at their images.

I wanted to know who they were and what they did, except it would delay finding out what I might be—and why I knew their faces.

As I was saying, Rainbow's people would help. Of this, she was certain. If Rainbow and Spring could get Torres back to the lands of what is now the Pueblos Naciones, they would find men and women willing to turn the tables upon their captor. To catch and imprison him until distance and lack of access to Spring's water in Rainbow's blood cause him to wither and die.

The matter, then, was to find a way to convince him to take them back.

What surer way than making him believe the Spring's power was fading?

At which point he stopped again, as dinner was served.

No matter how much my mouth watered at the sight and smell of barbecued meats and grilled vegetables, a heaviness started to grow in my stomach as though a lump lay there, though I hadn't taken a bite.

A lone breeze wound around me, stretching thin and yet somehow enveloping me. Energy pulsed through the air, in slow, steady succession. Each pulse rippled over my body without making any hair stand on edge. Which only served to unsettle me further.

This time, though, I waited all the way through dinner. Picked at my meal but didn't interrupt as Grampa and the others dug in with gusto. Then, at last, Jesse asked the question looming over all of us.

"How did Rainbow and Spring convince Torres the Spring's power had weakened?"

"The mystery of life." Grampa laughed.

There he went, being mysterious again. I looked down, so as not be caught rolling my eyes.

I mean this quite literally: the mystery of life which is birth.

Shortly after returning to Europe, Torres carried them away with him to the Netherlands, to East Frisia, in search of some treasure or other. A storm hit while they visited. The sea rose and flooded far and wide on Christmas night. Thousands died.

Rainbow and Spring were trapped in a house as the waters rose. Unfortunately for them, Torres was there too, but he paid little attention to the others in the dwelling. Not so Rainbow and Spring, for the pain and agony of a woman in labor called to them. They watched and helped as another servant tended the pregnant woman and delivered the baby. Both mother and child lived, but the mother took days to regain her strength.

In this, they found hope and inspiration. If they quickened and bore a child, they too might seem weakened.

They could pretend to dream that even as they labored in childbirth an earthquake rocked the lands where Spring once flowed free. That the earthquake loosened some measure of water to run there again, and thus less power flowed in their veins.

Of more import, they could suppress some measure of Spring's power after childbirth, enough to cause Torres to show some signs of age.

All this they plotted. It meant a major change, as they'd chosen not to bear children until then, but in the end they decided it was worth the risk.

My jaw hung wide open. I wasn't expecting that. Jesse, too, had a look of complete and total shock.

"So, Rainbow got pregnant to have an excuse to pretend she was weak and convince Torres that she no longer had as much power in her blood after the birth?" Just to be clear that I'd heard him right.

"Torres didn't know much about women." Hallemay gave a huff, shaking her head.

"He did not." Grampa nodded and took a sip of water. "Especially women he considered below his station. He enjoyed chasing ladies. Seducing them, though he lost interest after they gave in. He never paid much attention to servants or women who labored in villages and fields—except Rainbow. It was the lure of the seemingly unattainable he lusted after, above and beyond pleasures of the flesh. Though he still ordered her to his bed on occasion."

"And it worked?" I asked. "Having a baby?"

"At a cost." Grampa hunched over, head lowering. "Rainbow and Spring must have gone through agonies as they redirected as much of Spring's power as they could into other bodily fluids. Saliva, urine . . . the waters filling their womb, then the milk flowing from their breasts. They nursed their child, whom they loved more than they had anticipated, with milk of life. I told you the plan had flaws, not least that they gave Torres a hostage for their good behavior."

Last night's fragmented dream flashed through me. Once again, the arms of a woman who was my mother, even though she wasn't, wrapped around me. Cradled me. Rocked me.

"A few days after they gave birth, Torres came and took the child. He cut the infant and tasted the blood." Grampa ran his fingers along one arm, pushing his sleeve back to reveal a thin arm with muscles and sinews clear beneath the warm brown skin. "Then thrust the babe back into Rainbow's arms, complaining the blood was too weak to be any good."

"Little did he know." Grampa drained his glass, slurping the last drops of water.

Again my dreams flickered through me. Yet this one changed. Instead of being tied taut as string, my body jerked as though I were yanked from the warmth of cradling arms. A cold blade cut my arm, even as Grampa had drawn a line on his. Lips fastened and drank, then I was shoved back into welcoming arms.

"What happened to the baby?" The questions I really wanted to ask pressed on me, but giving voice would mean I couldn't call them back. The baby couldn't be me. I was Mom and Dad's child—Mom had pictures.

"He lives."

A wave of relief washed over me.

He, not she, not me.

No big conspiracy about me being somebody other than who I was. My imagination got wrapped up in the story and created the strange dreams. Or something like that, something sane and simple. Any explanation that didn't involve me having suppressed memories and a twisted past.

Then second word dawned. He *lives*. The child was still alive.

Grampa's head tilted downward. He drew aimlessly on the tablecloth.

"Rainbow knew better than to give her son a name that might betray her purpose in finding freedom, so she called him instead Ignacio."

Ignacio.

Grampa's name. Of course. That made such horrible sense.

He met my gaze and nodded, grip tightening on his cane.

"I am nearly three hundred years old, and I am tired. Tomorrow, when we find Torres, I need your help to finish this. It is not fitting that he live any longer."

GRAMPA'S TALE

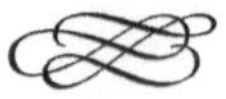

Everything changed. And yet it didn't. I couldn't process it all, what it meant.

For a three hundred years old man, he moved pretty spry even leaning on the cane. All the same, I had no problem giving up the front seat to him and shifting to the back again. So much more comfortable to be in my usual place, behind him, listening to the chair squeak as he shifted this way and that.

Nobody said anything at first. Hallemay headed us off west without asking Jesse to weigh in. Light poured into the car as overhead oranges, reds, and purples streaked the sky.

A little breeze danced around us, ruffling my hair one moment then Jesse's, but staying in the back away from Hallemay and Grampa.

Poor Jesse, having to take all this in a single day. He had a dazed look, head nodding as he drew in deep breath after deep breath.

But the day wasn't over.

"Go ahead and tell them the rest." Hallemay nudged Grampa, before returning her hand to the wheel.

"All of it?" He gave her a sharp glance.

"They need to know what they'll face tomorrow." She nodded her head and gestured to the west.

"Very well." He turned around in seat as best he could. His seat belt strained over his shoulder.

Despite the golden rays of the setting sun creating an aura behind him, his face became shadowed and paler than I'd ever seen. He stared right at me, dark eyes intent with undecipherable meaning.

"Keep your questions until another time, if you can. I must hoard my strength for tomorrow, and it is harder to tell the tale in chunks than whole cloth."

That stopped all the dozens of questions edging towards the tip of my tongue. I'd been good and held them back, in part because Hallemay had stared me down after Grampa's revelation of his birth, and Jesse gave me a nudge once or twice when I opened my mouth. Feet restless, I nodded.

To hear to the end, I'd sit on my questions one way or another.

Grampa leaned his head against the head rest and began again.

I was born for the purpose of helping free Rainbow and Spring. An after thought, as it were. Their plans centered upon using the after-effects of childbirth as a tool to free themselves. They expected to birth a healthy child, but did not anticipate how much they would love me. Or the ways Torres might use me as a means to ensure their cooperation and good behavior.

I do not know how to describe my childhood. Torres moved us every five to ten years and hired local servants until it was time to move on. He presented us as a family—father, mother, and child, and so I thought we were during my youth. You will likely not understand, but many families in those days, at least among the circles in which Torres preferred to socialize, were held together by things other than love. Money, land, business dealings. I recognized that Torres did not care for me, but he was not a loving man and I had few models for men who loved their children.

In my early years, Torres tried my blood to see if it had strengthened enough to sustain him. He stopped by the time I was five. All the same, nightmares plagued me for years. I called him Father, and rendered him due respect, but otherwise kept away from him as best I could.

Mothers, now . . . I always knew Rainbow loved me. You must remember, I did not then know Spring existed. Rainbow was most comfortable when I stayed close enough for her to see me hale and well.

He used that love—and me—against her. Let us leave it at that.

His voice grew thinner and his hands shook. He lowered his head, gazing down at the floor.

I laid my hand atop his where it gripped the seat back. His chilly skin made me hiss and jerk in shock. Gritting my teeth, I wrapped both hands around his.

Jesse reached out, too, and we each wound up with a hand to warm. Grampa's fingers moved within my grasp, but he didn't pull away and his skin seemed to warm, albeit slowly.

Perhaps it was Spring's influence, but when I grew old enough for schooling, I took an interest in medicine. This was despite Torres's preferences. He had little respect for doctors or surgeons, no matter he had once practiced medicine himself. Nevertheless, he gave me a sum of money and told me to find a way to support myself.

I used that to study medicine in Leiden. Sorry as I was to leave my mother, my years there were some of the best of my life. My innocence shielded me, and I thought only of my own hopes and desires.

Then a letter arrived from my mother.

She wanted me to know her love would never wane, her sorrow that we would not meet again, and sent prayers for my well-being. Apologizing for not having confided in me before, she wrote that she had convinced Torres to take her across the ocean to the Americas, where she was born—this I had not known until then—and did not expect to return.

To this day, I do not understand how she thought this would comfort me. Instead, it filled me with fear. I became increasingly aware of how harsh Torres used her.

From the vantage point of all I know now, his cruelty grew as Spring and Rainbow succeeded in withholding some measure of power. As gray streaked his hair, wrinkles sprouted on his face, and his bones began to creak, so he hurled scorn upon her and had no compulsion about hitting out with the back of a hand without caring if the blow sent her reeling.

Unaware of my mothers' plans, I resolved to follow. To help her escape, if she wanted.

Fortune and the ocean currents favored me. I arrived in the West Indies before they boarded a ship for Mexico. Though too late to arrange a cabin, I managed a place below deck.

My mother walked out in the air each day in company with the few other women travelers. Though I dared not venture near, I managed to encounter an older woman with a kind face, and convinced her to pass Mother a note asking what help she needed to ensure her safety.

The next time she took the air, she went forward to the bow. In the span of a moment, she managed to climb atop the railing and leap into the sea.

Grampa's fingers had warmed, though their touch still chilled me. His hand turned within mine and gripped hard. Tears trickled from his eyes, glittering in the last light of the sun as they trailed down his cheeks.

Then his face vanished as the last of the previous night's dreams reappeared before my eyes, this time at closer view. A seemingly young woman in a dress with flowing blue skirts whipped by the winds. She'd pulled her black hair into a loose knot atop her head. A few strands slipped loose to dance along her cheeks. She resembled Grampa, but even more she reminded me of Dad except shorter and slighter.

For one moment, she stood etched against the blue of sky and sea—then she was gone from sight.

"You don't have to . . . if it hurts . . ."

"No." He shook his head. "I'll see this through."

Before she leapt, my mother gave our confidante a letter for me. This was far more informative than her earlier. She recounted most of her history, knowing I would find it passing strange and possibly beyond comprehension.

I was not to fear for her, she told me. The waters of the Gulf would welcome her and bear her along her way back toward her homeland.

I should return to Europe, and when she had separated herself back into Spring and Rainbow, Rainbow would find some way to send me word.

But this I could not do. Leave her—them—to face it all alone? When I had already failed them, by not realizing how Torres held them captive?

"You never failed her." Hallemay pulled over in front of an inn. The building itself, a three-story mass of balconies and decorative trim, loomed high and dark. The oval light advertising vacant rooms paled to nearly nothing against the fiery bands of gold and red filling the horizon, from sky to hills and valleys, with warm color.

Releasing her seatbelt, which retracted with a loud snap, she turned and laid a hand around Grampa's shoulders. "She wanted you safe."

"Yes, I was a fool by some measures to follow." He drew in a shuddering breath. "But I loved her too much not to want to help."

"It's been a long day. Time to rest." She opened the door and a cool draft circled the car.

"They need to know what Torres is. You said so yourself."

"I can share that much, if you'll allow." Circling the car, she opened Grampa's door and helped ease him out. "You need your strength."

He didn't protest much, even when Hallemay refused to allow him to carry his own bag to one of the rooms she rented. Jesse carried half the bags, she took the rest. I got the honor of holding Grampa's arm and helping him climb the stairs, though he drew the line at any of us helping him get ready for bed.

Instead, Jesse and I followed Hallemay into the other room and took seats on one of the beds. She sat cross-legged on the other.

You can ask Grandfather for more details tomorrow, if you wish, but here is the bones of what you should know. The long and the short of it is, after the ship arrived in Veracruz he joined a caravan bound for Mexico City and then another up the Royal Road to Santa Fe.

He followed Torres—and Torres let him. What either thought they could do is beyond me. Grandfather had only the vaguest idea of where he headed and Torres, well, perhaps he believed he could come close enough to Rainbow and Spring to locate and track them.

Which, in the end, he did manage to do. I don't know how. Grandfather explained it to me three times and Grandmother once, but I still don't understand.

Their paths crossed in El Paso, for Rainbow and Spring followed the Rio Bravo, or Rio Grande if you prefer. The River helped them, but in the end they met up with Torres and Grandfather all the same.

And Torres used Grandfather as a lure—and a threat.

I don't know the exact details. Grandfather's tale is never quite the same twice. Somehow, they all wound up in the River: him, Torres, Rainbow, and Spring.

The River turned Torres into an alligator, then swept him away.

It took a while for that to sink in. I sat still, mouth gaping, and Jesse wasn't much better. That at least explained why Grampa learned to talk to alligators.

Hallemay allowed us a little time to adjust before cutting to the chase.

"The point being, what we face tomorrow is not a human, but an alligator. A man who has spent the last centuries as an alligator."

BLOOD TEARS

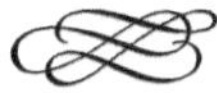

I tossed and turned that night, unable to get to sleep for ages. The mattress sank beneath me, too soft by far. Every movement sent ripples through the bedding until I might as well have wallowed in bathtub. The soft sheets had a slick side. The bottom was fine, giving way beneath me as I rolled over, but the top kept slipping off so I had to reach over and retrieve it from the carpeted floor.

At least my movements didn't disturb Hallemay. She snored away, lying still and somnolent in her bed.

If only that were me.

But how could I sleep with so much running through my brain?

I'd called Mom earlier to share news. She and Louie were fine, with Louie having no breathing problems or allergic incidents whatsoever. But when she asked how I was doing, though, I tried to figure out some way to sum up everything going on—and wound up weaseling out with little more than "I'm fine."

So much lay behind my fine, and so many unanswered questions. Every time Grampa answered one, he raised more.

I tried counting up what I didn't know but had to give it up. There was too much. Why had the River intervened, and how did it even have the power if none of the European rivers had helped? Where was Rainbow? Why had Grampa left Torres alone, as an alligator, all these years? How did he know where Torres-the-alligator was now and how had the alligator survived?

If Grampa was nearly 300 and Dad was his firstborn, when was Dad born?

Hallemay had always called me sister, and I'd thought it a courtesy. Especially after learning she'd passed her century. But if Dad were old enough to be her father, we could be sisters in fact, not just name.

What about me? Had the water of life changed their DNA and passed down to me to explain my rapid healing?

Only questions ran through my brain, until I finally fell asleep. Once again, my dreams didn't belong to me but someone else. Not Rainbow and Spring this time, though, but Grampa.

Jagged mountains rose before me, sharp against the darkening sky. Hard-baked earth lay below me. The leather of my shoes had worn thin, while my breeches and shirt went stiff from days of sweat and labor. Every muscle in my body ached. Warm lights shone here and there, where camp fires burned and people whispered—but most fires guttered. Better to seek one's bedroll early than stay up late only to stumble the next day.

A hint of moisture lingered in the air, for we'd crossed the river the day before and remained close enough to hear the water rushing on its way.

I should rest. My bedroll lay near, open and inviting even atop hard dirt.

Yet every time I moved toward it, breezes danced and tugged at my hair and sleeves.

This way, they seemed to say. Follow us.

If I closed my eyes, I fancied I heard my mother's voice bidding me listen and obey. Sneak away and meet her down by the river.

So I wandered there, not really believing although filled with enough hope for my heart to quicken its beat and blood flow fast through my veins. Glancing behind now and then, I saw nothing but shadows.

The breezes brought me to her—the mother I'd thought I knew.

And in that moment, I unwittingly betrayed her. My so-called father followed me. Oh, with the vantage of time and reason, I knew he had felt her presence in the way he had always used to track her. This did not alter the deep pang of pain in the moment at having found her bare minutes before he came.

But so too arrived animals by the score.

Snakes.

Hundreds, even thousands of them. All hissing as their long bodies entwined, disentangled, and shifted in a great curving mass that wove back and forth. The hisses grew in volume. Tongues flickered in the strong moonlight. Most were dark colors, but several were light brown with ruddy bands crossing their bodies. A heavy odor of musk filled the air, mingled with that of stagnant water.

Even Torres fell back rather than face their fangs. Back, and back, as Rainbow led me down into the river, which drew away from its banks.

The waters retreated, forming an alcove as we were herded onto rocks and weeds. With a roar, the waters resumed their course except where we stood. A perfect bubble surrounded us. Hundreds of fishes appeared, circling the bare spot and making a living wall of water and scales. The snakes topped the wall. More water arced overhead and the air within became so humid all were drenched. Hair drooped and clothes clung to bodies. No one spoke at first, for the moisture-heavy air made breathing difficult.

"You should never have stolen me or Spring," Mother said. "I give you this one chance, more than you ever gave to me. Let me go on my way, and you may go free on yours."

"I found it. Victori spolia." A strange ruddy light glinted as he drew a knife. "Your son's blood is too thin to protect him."

"You know nothing. Live, then, long enough you may regret."

With a harsh tug, she pulled me back against the living, pulsing wall of water and fish. A moment later, thick, foul-smelling sludge dripped from the roof of the chamber onto Torres. He thrashed, trying to keep his head clear, but the substance covered him. His back arched as he lost human form and reshaped into a short-legged, long-tailed alligator hissing and snapping in the center of the river bed.

Fish on upstream side of the wall holding back the river's full power opened a hole. Water gushed, sweeping Torres off his feet and dragging him through a matching hole on the downstream side.

I didn't wake, though. A new dream started instead.

I stood at the bow of a ship. Winds blew at my back, filling the air with the ocean brine. Gulls called overhead, their wings wide as they escorted us across the sea. I traveled alone, but with a great weight lifted from my shoulders even as a new responsibility rested on me. I would undo the evil the man I'd thought my father had wrought, and destroy his caches of ill-gotten spoils.

It helped that each new gust of wind at my back carried a fresh wave of reassurance.

"All's well," or, more precisely, "she's well."

Except, this dream morphed into another.

I knelt by the side of a stream. Tears trickled down my face, until my eyes grew sore from weeping.

The waters flowed before me, glinting in the sunlight. The perfume of mountain flowers filled the air, a scent that delighted me once upon a time for it represented a distillation of my mother. Rather, it was the second mother I'd not known or realized existed.

On whose banks I collapsed in grief and regret. The spring shifted its path, spilling over one hand. The smooth current running over my skin roused rills of ease.

When I wiped my face, my other hand came away dripping with ruddy liquid, for my tears were red as blood.

HUNTING TORRES

*H*unting an alligator proved far more complicated than I had imagined. We needed permits. Not one but two, since the free city of El Paso and the Apacheria shared governance of this side of the river. Who knew? Not me, since I'd never hunted anything larger than a mouse or over-large spider.

All of which meant we didn't get out to the river until midday. The sun shone high and hot overhead. A thin layer of sweat already made my T-shirt stick to the small of my back, especially since I had on a blue jacket which soaked up sunlight. My pants likewise were hot, but the thick jean fabric of jacket and pants should give me some protection. I wore hiking boots Mom had insisted on buying. The hard-ridged soles sank when I made the mistake of stepping near a sandy spot, but mostly sent pebbles and rocks skittering as I strode over hard-baked earth.

A few trees bent and swayed in a rising breeze—a willow here and several wide overgrown, thorny bushes Grampa called honey mesquite. The wealth of shrubs made up for the lack of trees. Some bore bright flowers in yellows and reds, and all had ample spiky leaves or thorns. Sage and other savory scents I couldn't identify reached me. The plants grew close to the river, where the earth was softer.

As for the river itself, it matched my dream for width and depth. Light sparkled off ripples and waves as water rushed downward. At least it behaved as most rivers, with no walls of fishes and snakes. I kept a careful eye out for snakes.

"There was a good snow-pack in the mountains this last winter." Grampa studied the river, nodding his head. "It's good to see the river running strong."

He, Hallemay, and Jesse also wore thick pants and jackets over their shirts, and hard-soled shoes. I stuck out, though, because my jeans were plain blue, a bit faded at the knees and elbows. Jesse wore leather that carried a faint smoky scent. A mix of greens and browns, in dancing swirls, marked Hallemay's clothes.

Grampa had brown painted with black and red swoops, except where a thick belt around his waist held a long sheath. He'd drawn the sword as soon as we left the car, and carried it with both hands wrapped around the long handle. I'd expected the blade to flash in the light, but it didn't. The metal had a slightly dull tinge to it, except now and then a shadow flitted along its length.

Even without warning, I stayed well away from Grampa.

My hands wrapped around his regular walking stick. Despite the zigs and zags, it had a great balance. The long handle contained a dagger with six-inch blade that Grampa showed me how to detach if I needed something sharper. I kept my hand wrapped around it, ready to hit out or slip under.

Because that was my and Jesse's role in this fight. Jesse carried another of Grampa's walking sticks, this one half again as long as the one I had and a lot thicker, plus a lariat. Ideally, Jesse would lasso one of Torres's limbs so we could get the sticks under and use our weight to flip him over. Then Grampa could slice his belly with the sword. Or Hallemay shoot him. Or both.

"A slug or two down the gullet should slow him down," she'd said earlier as she strapped a pistol at her waist, then picked up a shotgun. She wasn't sure the pistol would kill as fast and sure as the shotgun. They were meant for crazed animals or evil humans, not humans turned into alligators. "He hasn't had water of life in centuries, so he's mortal."

"Should be," Grampa nodded. "But he's lasted this long on the water he drank. If he gets a whiff, he'll want a taste again."

At which they both turned toward me. Jesse didn't, instead glancing back and forth between them. Nice to have company in my ignorance, for once.

"He won't recognize me." Grampa said. "Nor Hallemay nor Jesse, but let him get a whiff of you, Mara, and he'll come running for a taste."

"You want to explain that?" My blood didn't run cold, but every muscle quivered. There it was, out in the open, but still no reason, no story, no end in sight.

"Soon, but now's not the time." Grampa shifted the sword to one hand and wrapped his other around me, pulling me close. "You're the best lure for getting him up and away from the river, where he's slower, but don't get close to his mouth and teeth, whatever you do."

"Wasn't planning on it." Try as I might, I couldn't stay stiff in his embrace. "Don't you let him get you either."

By the time he let me go, Hallemay and Jesse formed an advance line heading down toward the river where Grampa thought Torres lurked.

The breezes flitting around me blew stray images of an immense alligator in the water—broken and out of order with no real sense of where he lay. Among reeds. Clambering along a river bank. Amidst swaying stalks.

I started after them, but Grampa grabbed my arm.

"There!"

Too late, I whirled to find a blur of scaled legs and body whipping across the ground faster than I'd have thought possible. All those breeze-blown images of a giant alligator? Nothing compared to the real thing: a three-meter, four-or-five-hundred kilogram scaled creature barreling our way.

Grampa was wrong, though. Torres didn't run at me, but him. His thick legs ended in stubby digits and sharp claws that glittered and cast up gouts of dirt with each forward step.

The sword caught the sunlight, nearly blinding me, as Grampa swung. The blade hit the massive snout with a thwack.

Torres kept going, aiming for Grampa.

Ran into him.

Over him.

Grampa lashed out with the sword a second time, then shrieked as he toppled. Crumpled.

Torres turned to run back over him.

"Help! Help!" I drew the dagger, holding it in my right hand, and the twisted wood cane in my left. Hallemay and Jesse turned and started running back, but they were so far away.

Torres's head swung back and forth. His snout opened and he bellowed.

And ran at me.

The bitter taste of copper flooded my mouth. My lungs hurt and heart beat faster than a butterfly's wings.

I stood my ground until the last moment. Darting aside, I swung the cane at his snout and aimed the dagger at his eyes. Those few points he might be vulnerable.

Sharp pangs bloomed along my leg as he snapped at me.

Whirling around, I lashed out again and again. The cane hit the ground once, sending painful vibrations up my arms.

I hit my mark more often than not.

Snout.

Snout.

Eyes, though with the cane, not the dagger.

Snout.

Then the tail whipped around and knocked me down.

Cane and dagger flew from my hands. I hit the ground with a grunt, then lay still. Breath gone from my lungs until I heaved and drew in a great gulp.

A breeze brought the image of Torres, jaws gaping wide, aiming for my arm.

I rolled, over and over until I hit something that groaned.

Grampa.

His legs were a mess, bleeding through great rents in the fabric. His arms wrapped around me, grip tightening for a moment.

Then he pushed me out of the way.

Torres trampled him again, this time his feet digging into Grampa's chest. No matter how thick, the cloth ripped beneath sharp claws.

"*No!*" I flailed, but a gust of air guided one hand to metal. Grabbing the sword, I hacked at Torres.

He opened his jaw wide and turned toward me.

Something cracked and whistled in the distance as Torres approached.

Then retreated. Shifted back centimeter by centimeter.

One meter away.

Two.

Three.

In the distance, Jesse and Hallemay pulled on the rope fastened around Torres's tail. Jesse wrapped the other end around a tree, tying it tight.

Torres fought. Bellowed. His sharp claws scored the earth, sending clumps flying.

Hallemay picked up her shotgun and aimed it down Torres's wide jaw. A deep crack resounded through the air. Torres jerked, then bellowed and snapped his snout shut.

But still fought the rope. Though stout, the tree swayed.

Pain ripped along my legs, but I pushed myself up. Grabbed the sword, might've leaned on it for a moment.

Jesse got his cane wedged under Torres and tried to flip him. Thick as the wood was, it didn't go anywhere.

The damn beast was just too big and heavy.

But I had a sword that once belonged to El Cid, or so Grampa had said. Was it magic? Maybe not. Or maybe.

All the same, I swung it up.

Torres's eyes fixed on me.

Then I plunged the pointy end down with all my might. Scales flew, but the sword only went in a little way.

I lifted the sword again. A second pair of hands wrapped around mine, and a strong body braced me.

"On the count of three," Jesse said.

Down the blade came again. Scales parted, flesh burned. The beast gave a last bellow.

He thrashed. The force knocked Jesse and me both backward. I landed atop him, just far enough away to watch as Hallemay aimed her shotgun at Torres's open maw and from less than a meter away sent another bullet rocketing through his body.

The beast died.

Breezes surrounded him, whipping his scales away and transforming the ancient, overgrown alligator back into an aged man. A mass of wrinkles and long, unkempt white hair. The body then turned to dust and blew away.

The sword hit the ground with a dull clang.

Torres was dead.

What about Grampa?

Legs aching, I stumbled over the ground and fell to my knees at Grampa's side. Bright red streaked his chest and legs, soaking his shirt and pants. His lips barely moved, but he still breathed.

"Torres?"

"Dead." My hands hovered over him, trembling. I didn't know what to do to help. Anything I touched, except maybe his head, had to hurt.

"Good."

Thuds and loud panted breaths, then Hallemay and Jesse dropped down beside me.

"Go get water," Hallemay said to Jesse. "And bring a shirt or something soft, a clean rag."

He took off, turning into a blur in the haze. I started to stand, but a rip of pain in my legs dropped me back. Pulling sticky cloth away from my legs, I checked some of the claw marks. The wounds had started to heal, but remained red and swollen.

"You stay here until your legs have healed more. No sense making things worse." Hallemay stroked Grampa's cheek with the back of a hand. "Torres is gone, Grandfather. It's done."

"Good." A shiver rippled through his body. His grabbed at her, fingers catching her sleeve and then his hand fell back. "Patch me. Don't make her lose me. Children should never die before parents. Keep me . . . going . . . long enough."

"Of course." She ripped his shirt and pulled the cloth to the side.

Torres had walked over Grampa, at least twice stomping so heavily his claws dug deep and tore as he moved on. Several of the jagged, gaping holes were as big as any of my finger tips.

Grampa still breathed.

I'd taken much less damage, but my wounds had closed. Ripples of energy raced along the length of my legs, so frenetic I could probably spark static electricity in the middle of a rainstorm. My blood no longer flowed free, slowing to a mere ooze.

Not so Grampa. He kept bleeding.

Jesse came crashing down next to us, with several full bottles of water and a couple of shirts.

Hallemay grabbed one bottle. Opening it, she poured water of life over Grampa's wounds until they ran pink instead of red.

"I have a phone, back at the car. Satellite phone. We can call for help."

"That'll come in handy, but not now. We need to stabilize him. Get water of life into him anyway we can, so it keeps him going."

Jesse tore the shirts into wide strips. I soaked them in water from the other bottles. Hallemay laid them on Grampa's wounds.

He gasped and hissed, body arching, then went limp.

A cry escaped me, but Hallemay gave me a sharp look.

"No time for that. He lives. We have to keep him that way." She pulled out the car keys and tossed them next to Jesse. "Bring the car as close as you can. We have to get him in and get on the road."

He ran off again, leaving me to rip cloth and soak them in water. Bit by bit, Grampa's bleeding slowed. But the wounds didn't close.

Scabs already covered the gashes on my legs. Water of life ran in my blood, one way or another.

Maybe, I could share with Grampa?

"Would . . . would my blood help?"

"How so?" Hallemay pressed dripping pad of cloth against the deepest hole.

"I heal fast and . . . Torres drank from Rainbow, so—"

Her startled eyes met mine, then she shook her head.

"No, Mara. Even if it could work, Grandfather would refuse. No."

I held sopping cloth against Grampa's leg, torn at not being able to help him no matter how much I hadn't wanted to feed him my blood, or what that would mean.

"We have to get him to a spring of life." Hallemay said, and sighed. "The Great Roads are fastest, so for once we'll take them. We'll make it to Santa Fe by twilight, if all goes well, and to Spring well before midnight."

The rumble of the car tires grinding closer over the rocky ground nearly obscured her last words.

"You'll get to meet Spring."

My jaw dropped and every nerve in my body jangled. We headed not merely to a spring of life but *that* spring.

MEETING SPRING

Driving on a Great Road meant a much smoother ride. The tires rolled over a straighter surface. Though there were still hills and valleys and turns, and too often the curves or going uphill or downhill meant Grampa got jostled. He groaned a lot.

I kept my own groans to myself. Not that I had much to moan about. The worst for me wasn't that bad. I still wore my ripped jeans, and fabric, stiff with my blood, scraped my legs constantly. That was all. My wounds had healed long ago.

And it was nothing to watching Grampa fade.

We'd rearranged the car before leaving, putting down the seat back so Grampa lay mostly flat, with me perched next to him. Sometimes hunching and dangling my legs off the end behind the front seats, and other times lying next to Grampa trying to keep him steady. The smell of blood and the faint floral perfume of water of life mixed together, hitting the back of my throat and almost triggering my gag reflex.

I had one task: keep the cloths resting on his wounds damp. Whenever one started drying out, I swapped it with another soaked in water of life, always keeping one soaking in a makeshift bowl.

At least, I'd do this as long as the supply of water of life lasted.

The tank had shrunk as small as it would go. The collapsed frame made it hard to see how much was left, but the way it sloshed around sounded smaller. It was getting low.

The occasional sign posted next to the Road gave the only indication of where we were—except for the big sign welcoming us to the Pueblos Naciones in gold letters against a dark mountain backdrop. I knew better than to bother Jesse or Hallemay by asking how much longer. The expressions on their faces the one time I'd tried . . . not encouraging.

The last sign had advertised the next exit as Santa Fe.

The road kept climbing and curving around between hills. Tall, resonant blue-green mountains rose in the distance. White patches marked the upper sides of one or two peaks, clouds probably but possibly snow. Closer by, the hard-baked ground split into twisted gullies and canyons. Scrubby bushes grew, sharp and thorny in varying greens that stood out against dull brick red earth.

Jesse drove most of the time. Nobody offered me a chance, and just as well since I hadn't a clue how to drive or where to go or both. But he managed an even pace while trying to avoid any sudden speeding up or slowing down.

Hallemay took over my phone almost the whole time, except when the power ran out and she had to hold it up to the sun to refresh the battery. The sun still shone, but kept creeping closer to the horizon.

Most of her calls she made in the same strange language Grampa used the other night, though she didn't speak it as well as he. Every now and then, she threw in a word in

English or Spanish, not that those gave me any idea what she said.

Grampa, on the other hand.

He muttered to himself a lot. Not sentences, just fragments.

"Return it." His head rolled to the side, eyes closed. "Not yours. Wrong. Evil."

"Easy, Grampa." I replaced the cloth on his upper chest with a new one. "We got Torres. Just take it easy now."

"Come back. Carlito. One tear, that's all. No!" He tried to sit up, only to give a croak of pain.

I had just enough time to slip an arm behind him and ease his slump back down onto the car bed.

"Don't leave." He moaned. "Come back."

At which point for a moment he blinked and recognized me.

"Mara, you'll cry for me?"

"Hold on." My fingers gripped his hand as I pressed the damp cloth against the blood seeping from his wounds.

He pressed back, but only for a moment and then he started babbling again. "My blood, in my blood all the time. Didn't know. My mistake. Made things worse. The children carry it. We're all wrong. Must set it right. She's dying."

And on and on, as the sun sank lower in the sky, and the car grew cooler.

All at once city lights appeared in a valley ahead. The sun hadn't set but twinkling points appeared against the dark the hills.

"Take the next exit, then pull to the side." Hallemay told Jesse.

Within moments after he left the Great Road and reached a regular one, the rougher surface sent additional vibrations through the car. Grampa gave a low moan.

"I know this section well." Hallemay took over the driver's

seat, swapping with Jesse. She took the roads fast, twists and turns and all, sending us climbing into the hills.

I kept hold of Grampa. He stopped babbling, but not in a good way. His body lay limper than before, his hands loose at his side and head rolling until I braced it between my duffle bags.

"Hurry."

Hallemay cast a glance over her shoulder, then looked at Jesse. He twisted around, touched Grampa's cheek, and nodded to Hallemay.

Who sped up—because we headed downhill. Not a simple straight shot, but a winding track back and forth as we seemed to lose nearly all the height we'd gained. The mountains disappeared, hidden behind steep, rocky canyon walls, and everything grew darker as we moved away from the setting sun.

The pavement gave way to gravel.

Then we entered a clearing and came to a stop. Trees and bushes grew around, but far enough from each other for the rocky slopes to be visible through them. The thickest greenery lined the banks of a narrow creek.

Three cars, including a road runner just like Hallemay's except painted bright purple and gold, and a truck sat parked in a neat line.

Nearby stood a cluster of people. A lantern glowed from atop the other road runner, and a second dangled from one of the people's hands. They kept moving, making it hard to figure out just how many there were.

No sooner had we come to a stop than they circled the car. High and low voices called out in English, Spanish, and the language I didn't know and still hadn't recognized.

Hallemay and Jesse got out of the car, rocking it a little as they did, and out of the way.

Grampa moaned, a shudder rippling through his body.

An older man with gray-flecked black hair leaned in. Thin gray eyebrows rose high and he hissed, running one finger alongside a steep nose. Then he brought out a silver-toned flask, bright against the warm bronze-brown of his skin.

"Hold his head for me."

I didn't recognize his accent. It reminded me a little of Grampa and Dad, but he didn't pronounce the words quite the same. Didn't make much difference, the command had me snapping to.

The stranger pulled the top off the flask, and a wondrous scent filled the air for a moment. A faint hit of wildflowers soothed the back of my nose and throat, same as I was used to with the water of life but a thousand, a million, times stronger. The very act of inhaling invigorated every muscle and sinew in my body. As though I'd just taken a breath of the purest air imaginable—and been eased into a warm, soothing bath at the same moment.

Drop after drop fell from the flask into Grampa's mouth, as I held it open. After the first few, he sighed. Another, and he licked his lips, and the stranger lowered the flask so Grampa could drink more deeply.

The car shifted a little as Hallemay watched from the open door behind the stranger. She shivered and sagged against the frame.

On the other side, some of the weariness in Jesse's face drained away. He murmured something I didn't catch, but the stranger evidently did.

"Yes, water fresh from the spring. Gathered a few hours ago." The stranger gave Jesse a lopsided smile that twisted to the left and gave my heart a sudden twang.

Grampa opened his eyes to stare at the man, who pulled the flask back. They exchanged smiles, the same on each face and twisting to the same side.

They both had Dad's smile.

The stranger caught me staring and smiled at me. Then he drew back and let two young men ease Grampa out onto a litter. A woman settled at Grampa's side with another man, checking his wounds, while a fourth man was on a phone and another woman talking with Hallemay and Jesse. They were presumably from one of the Pueblos Naciones, but no one said anything indicating which.

The older man helped me out of the car, still smiling at me with Dad's smile.

"You must be Mara." He swept me into a hug. His arms wrapped close, but not too tight, and his chin brushed my temples. Pulling away, albeit with an arm still around me, he called over shoulder to Grampa. "She doesn't look at all like you!"

"Who're you?"

"This is my youngest." Grampa waved a hand, looking better but still pale and frail. Blood seeped from his leg wounds, but they had begun to scab over. "Your Uncle Antonio and some of his family. They're Cochiti, as was Antonio's mother and mine, and these are their ancestral lands."

So many new family members. All seemed delighted to meet me even in such hard circumstances. For a moment my head whirled with introductions to cousin this and cousin that, but Uncle Antonio put a stop to it with a shake of his head.

"There'll be time for this later, but the light's already gone. We need to get on our way."

The youngest of the men took up either end of the litter. A woman carrying a lantern took the lead. Others carrying lanterns stayed near the litter-bearers to light their steps.

I fell in line next to my new-found uncle as we started off on a path alongside the creek bed.

At least, it seemed to be a path, but not one I could have ever found on my own. Breezes blew leaves and pine needles off the ground to line a clear route. The earth rumbled beneath our feet as dirt shifted to make our way smooth. Trees sent their roots deeper, or pulled them back and out of our way.

When I glanced back, the ground moved back to its earlier appearance. Any signs of footsteps vanished, and air spirits blew pine needles and leaves back over the earth.

Hallemay accompanied the woman leading the way. They seemed well acquainted, for they conducted a low conversation complete with the occasional glance my way.

Uncle Antonio stayed close to the litter. Whenever the trail was wide enough, he held Grampa's hand. When it wasn't, he fell back into step with me.

"It is a delight to meet you at last. Father's told us stories about visiting you for years, and all of my children and grandchildren are looking forward to meeting you. Though I admit the younger are entranced at the idea of having a cousin in a place as strange and faraway as Philadelphia. They will be after you for details, but never fear. Your aunt or I will rescue you whenever you require."

I couldn't guess his age, but if he had grandchildren near my age, he was older than I'd thought.

My father had siblings. I'd known of other relatives beyond Grampa and Hallemay, but no idea of the scope. I thought maybe a handful, but my new uncle mentioned two sisters and their families, in addition to his own.

"I didn't know. Grampa didn't tell me about all of you."

"Well, he would not. He wanted time with you first. And it is true there are some among us, and not just the youngest, who are not the best at keeping secrets. We understood Grampa wouldn't bring you here until you were ready to return the last water of life."

"Until I what?"

"Return the stolen water of life. The drop in your blood, inherited from Carlos." Antonio shook his head as the trail took a turn. "Poor Carlos. I met him only once, and he ran from me. Father said when he first learned of your existence that this would bring the circle to an end. Carlos refused to return his drop, but surely you would be willing to give back yours."

Stolen water of life was in my blood. I could accept that. I already had, to some degree. Inherited from my father, which I had guessed.

I was to give it back? Grampa expected this of me, although he'd never said as much.

"We hadn't got to that part of the story yet." Grampa twisted on the litter, reaching back towards me.

That part of the story. It wasn't just a tale to get me to hunt Torres with him. The water in my blood was part of the story.

"My blood. Is that . . . all . . . you wanted of me?"

The trail widened enough for both me and Uncle Antonio to walk alongside the litter. He nudged me along, close enough for Grampa to grab my hand. His skin seemed hot to the touch, or maybe I'd just gone cold.

"Not your blood, but the water in it." He shook his head, gaze fixed on me. "I was born with water of life in my veins. Stolen water. It is a wrong thing, tainted. The only thing to do is to give it back to Spring. I didn't realize it in time, before the births of my first children, and passed it to them. Tainted them. We all must give it back."

"That's why you came, after Dad died." The pieces began falling into place. "Why you had the paternity test. You only wanted to find me because I was his daughter, carried his blood. That's all you've ever wanted."

I shivered, breath coming in pants. Grampa's fingers

clutched at me, but I pulled away. Backed away until I hit a tree trunk. The procession slowed as Grampa lurched and tried to grab at me. Everyone slowed, stopped, and turned to stare at us. At me.

He'd wanted my blood—no, the water in it.

Not me.

All his caring, the memories of our visits, turned to ash and dust in my mouth. They were nothing but a pretense. Grampa hadn't wanted to meet me. He'd wanted to get something from me, the water my father had refused to return.

Uncle Antonio said something, at least his mouth moved. So did Grampa and maybe someone else, but I couldn't hear anything but my heart beating and lungs panting.

Couldn't bear all the eyes staring at me.

I had to get away.

I didn't care where we were, how strange or dangerous. Foolish. Reckless. None of that mattered.

Turning, I ran off into the woods.

Voices sounded behind me, but the same power that cleared the trail for the litter also made way for me and let me slip into the wilderness.

I wouldn't have gone far, not really. I wasn't that stupid. All I needed was a few moments away, to myself, to mourn the loss of believing Grampa cared for me as me, not because he wanted something from me.

Then the light evening breezes blowing around me tugged me away, farther from the creek trail. Trees and bushes bent around me, making a shelter for a moment.

The earth beneath my feet heaved and my body jerked.

The next moment, I was far away.

Everything had changed.

The trees and bushes vanished, along with the creek and path and people carrying the litter.

I couldn't see Uncle Antonio or Jesse anywhere.

Or Hallemay.

Or Grampa.

Yet everything that met my eyes seemed vaguely familiar. I froze in place and closed my eyes. Drew in deep breath after deep breath until my breathing settled and my heart slowed to something closer to its normal pace.

Cool breezes danced around me, whispering my name. Behind them came the soft chime of water dripping over rocks.

Every breath carried the familiar smell of flowers. This time not diffuse, as in the older water of life, or so strong and concentrated as with the water Uncle Antonio gave Grampa. All the same, the scent alone eased a little of my sorrow.

Opening my eyes, I turned around and stopped at the soft reflection of moonlight on water seeping out from a rocky cliffside to trickle and form pools as it wound its way through a clearing. Small purple flowers bloomed along its banks. Grasses of varying heights swayed in the breeze, as they danced on the earth.

I'd seen this in my dreams. It struck a chord in my heart. A feeling of home equal to that of being embraced by my mother or Louie. Or, until most recently, Grampa or Hallemay.

With a soft chime, the water ceased trickling. Instead it lifted and took human shape, colorless save for the silvery moonlight. About my height, rivulets rippled over shoulders. The watery image stretched out its hands and mine reflex-ively rose to meet them.

The touch of its water on my skin sent reverberations through me. I dropped to the ground. Curled up in a ball, with my arms over my chest, and rocked back and forth. Warmth infused my body as Spring cradled me at the edge of its banks.

THE LAST DROP

I don't know how long I lay there, with water and warmth surrounding me. The scent of flowers filling the air as breezes touched my cheeks and flitted through my hair. Soft grasses shifted to cushion the ground. Every lingering ache vanished.

Yet I remained drained and unable to summon the will to move.

The water and warmth retreated, leaving me cool and damp but not soaked.

A very human hand stroked my back.

Uncurling into a seated position, I glanced around. Hallemay sat next to me. The moonlight shifted her face into sharp planes and shadows.

She swept a finger under each of my eyes, a gentle touch that found no dampness or sign of tears.

"Our father taught you well not to cry." Settling back and she dipped a hand into the spring.

"Our father."

"I told you, when we first met, that it was complicated but

to think of me as a big sister." She stretched her hands out to either side. "Sometimes the easiest thing is to tell the truth, even if you don't expect to be believed."

"You're my sister."

Hallemay still had her hands out, palms gleaming in the light from the moon and reflections off the water. I didn't want to get her wet, but I put my hands in hers and squeezed. Next thing, she hugged me close, squeezing tight enough to wring a few drops from my shirt.

When she pulled back, her eyes were damp.

"Why didn't he ever mention you?" I clapped a hand over my mouth, as I put the pieces together. If Dad was her father, he'd bought her freedom but left her with her enslaved mother.

Of course he wouldn't have told me.

"Sorry." I ducked my head then looked up to meet her eyes as I apologized. "I guess he wasn't ever much of a father to you."

"Not as he was to you," she said. "Maybe he changed. I saw him once a year as a child, then not at all for years until our roads crossed a few decades back. After that, we met up now and then, every other year or so as little more than strangers."

Leaning forward, she touched the dry skin under my eyes again. I flinched, and she drew back.

"When I was little, he told me not to cry, just as he did you. He never told me why. Then Grandfather discovered my existence and tracked me down."

Grampa's betrayal flashed through me anew. The soft ground squelched beneath me as I shuffled backward, widening the gap between us. Grampa hadn't acted alone.

She noticed but didn't mention my moving or follow behind me.

"Grandfather told me the story much as he did you, in bits and pieces. Fits and starts. Then he brought me here—I was older than you are now—and explained what it was that flowed in my veins." She dipped her fingers into the spring again, and tendrils of water twined around them.

Another tendril of water trickled from the spring to wrap around my ankle. I had arms tight over my chest, but the soothing warmth of the water seeped up to ease my tension. I followed Hallemay's example, letting one hand trail in the spring—and Spring held my hand as well as water could.

"Those of us with water of life in our blood do not age physically beyond full growth. Our progress to full growth is slow and we reach maturity late." She shrugged, flashing me a half-smile. "I didn't go through puberty and have my first period until I was thirty. You'll probably be much the same."

My mouth gaped open, and a breeze blew it shut with a click. I hadn't expected that—my small size and physical immaturity, over which Mom worried so and consulted so many specialists, all due to the very thing that kept me healthy despite the rest.

"You're eighteen. Law and custom consider you of age, but you have yet to fully mature." Hallemay raised her eyebrows and paused, giving me room to speak.

An owl hooted in the distance, but I kept silent.

"This does not mean you cannot understand what we are —and what is at stake." She said. "Grandfather was born with water of life in him, from both parents. He drew in more water of life as he nursed. But what ran in his veins, and what he passed down to his descendants until he realized and gave it up, was very different from that which flowed in Rainbow. It is a perverted reflection."

"Okay." My hands clenched into fists. Tendrils of water slipped through my immersed hand, coaxing it back open so rivulets might run over my palm. I kept my other closed, but not so tightly.

"We are what Torres wanted to be." Hallemay leaned forward, eyes catching the light and flashing despite the growing dark of night. "The water of life in our veins sustains us, keeping us young and healthy—but it helps only us. It is a corrupted version of true water of life, which helps any and all."

The words sank in, but their meaning took longer to register. I had to parse through each part of what she said and add it back up to make a whole.

It didn't add up.

"You say we. But . . . do you have water of life in your blood?" I scanned her face, noting the wrinkles and gray hairs that had contributed to me not seeing her as my sister for so long.

"I did when I was born, and until my late twenties, but not anymore. I returned it to Spring, where it belongs. As did Grandfather, long before Uncle Antonio's birth. As has everyone in the family who was born with water of life in their veins except our father . . . and you."

There we were, back to the reason I'd run. It hurt as much now as then, a tightening in my chest despite Spring's warmth and care.

"If you give it back, you will still age slower and likely live longer than most others. I've lived more than a hundred years without water of life in my veins. All the same, there will be days you will regret it." Her face twisted and she drew in a slow, halting breath. Tears trickled from her eyes. "I regret. Often. If I had not returned the water of life, then my daughter would have it in her veins and would not need to risk her life to carry a child to term."

"I'm sorry."

A nod, then she sighed.

"But returning the stolen drops was the right thing to do. My regrets do not outweigh surety that it was right. There are so many wrongs in this world, still. We cannot undo the thefts of Rainbow and the Spring, but we can at least refuse to profit and live indefinitely extended lives." Hallemay pulled her hand from the spring and held it suspended as drops fell back into the running water. "And so, as Grandfather asked me, I ask you to return that which was stolen."

"Of course." I sniffed. "It's all you want."

"How so?"

"Grampa only tracked me down because I was Dad's child." My hand remained immersed in water. Spring understood, or so it seemed, and comforted me. "Getting the water back was all that mattered, not me."

"What are you talking about?" Hallemay shook her head. "Mara, if the water were all Grandfather cared about, he could have had it from you when we first tracked you down. I saw your face that day. If he'd asked you for the moon you'd have tried to give it to him. But he didn't ask. Not then. He wanted time with you, to know you. To love you. He waited until now, until you were of age and even so he might have waited longer—fearing you'd run from him as his son did—because he loves you."

I dropped my gaze, watching ripples in moonlight instead of her face. My head whirled, trying to reconcile all the different parts of the tale, the various motives, into one coherent whole.

Grampa waited because he loved me?

"But he also loves his mother, Rainbow, as do I. I agreed to accompany Grandfather as much because she asked as for him, or you." Hallemay said. "We both want her to know the last drop was restored before she dies."

The owl hooted once more. A moment later, voices sounded in the distance along with the uneven beat of footsteps. The crack of twigs breaking beneath human weight. Golden light filtered through the trees, slowly filling the clearing as people bearing lanterns preceded those carrying Grampa's litter.

They approached on the opposite side of Spring, so I had ample time to watch their arrival.

Bushes parted to let them through. Everyone kept back except the two litter-bearers, now Uncle Antonio and Jesse. They laid the litter close by the spring, then retreated— although each glanced at me or Hallemay, or both.

Grampa lay still. His chest rose and fell with regular breaths, but he didn't move much. He turned his head and held out a hand.

That was enough.

Spring rose in human form and bent over Grampa. Water dripped from its hands into his mouth. The soft slurp of his drinking was the only sound for a few moments. Then he reached up to cup a hand around a watery cheek.

"Thank you, other Mother."

The water returned to flow in its usual course. He wavered as he sat up. Chest rose and fell in a deep breath. He stood and glanced around, only to stop and stare at me.

Agony shone clear on his face. Unmistakable even half in shadow.

He'd given me time to learn to love him before risking my hatred. How had I repaid him? By making him relive Dad running from him.

Yanking my hand from the water, I stood and leaped over Spring to throw myself at him. He caught me, staggering but his arms wrapped tight, and he returned my embrace.

"I'm sorry. Sorry, sorry, sorry."

Both of us tripped over our tongues to apologize, until we stopped and took a breath at the same time. Only to burst into relieved laughter. My fingers wrinkled his shirt and his dug into my back, then he pulled back slightly.

"I never wanted you to run from me." He held my head between hands as warm as Spring's water.

"I didn't understand."

"Now you do?"

"I understand more," I said. "That you waited to ask me until I was of age."

"I would have come to meet you even if you weren't Carlos's daughter by blood. Because you mattered to him, you were family, and part of what was left after he died." He rested his forehead against mine. "I loved you as my grandchild from the first moment I saw you."

"Love you too, Grampa." I hugged him and got squeezed in return.

Then he pulled back and swallowed hard.

"I would have waited longer, but you are the only remaining human with the water of life in your blood. And my mother is dying. Will you return the last drop to Spring?"

The weight of the story pressed on me. I'd lived a sliver of what Rainbow and Spring went through, and never would know the whole. Wouldn't have to live with anything close to their horror and pain.

Hallemay was probably right that I'd regret either way. I sort of understood Dad not wanting to give up something that had been part of him from the first. But it was stolen, and wrong to keep.

"How do I give it back?"

Grampa brushed a finger down my cheek.

Of course. What had Dad taught me never to do?

Before either of us could move, a new wave of footsteps

broke the quiet. Bushes at the far end of the clearing parted, letting person after person through. Old and young. Tall and short. Most in T-shirts, jackets, and pants, but some wearing skirts or dresses or long, flowing shirts.

A few whispered or spoke in low voices as they formed row after row circling the clearing. Children stood in front of parents. Some carried babies and infants in their arms.

Many weeping.

An older woman made her way around the circle to stand next to Uncle Antonio.

Behind her came two men carrying a litter. They bent and gently laid it on the earth near the spring. With a nod to Grampa, they retreated to join the others.

Spring again took human form, but this time raised a hand in greeting rather than reach out.

Did not offer healing, only comfort.

Grampa led me over to kneel next to the litter.

An old woman rested in a nest of woven blankets. A long braid of pure white hair looped across her body. It rose and fell, but barely. Her every breath was shallow. Small and slight, no bigger than me, a mass of wrinkles formed her face. A fading light shone in her eyes.

Grampa kept an arm around me even as he took her hand.

Hallemay joined us.

Drawing a deep breath, I let go. My eyes blazed. Pressure built and mini-lightning strikes flickered, turning everything shades of red.

Dryness gave way to dampness.

I wept.

With Rainbow's eyes on me, Spring leaned in and swept a watery hand across my face—carrying away tears of blood and leaving healing in their place.

I kept crying, though now my tears ran clear. All the

sorrows of the evening, and the pain of Dad's loss, drained away, leaving me cleansed and whole.

We all stood witness as Rainbow died knowing the last drop of stolen water of life had returned to the spring.

THE END.

MORE TALES OF THE TWISTING WORLD!

Be among the first to learn of new releases: sign-up for her newsletter at https://BookHip.com/PCSWMCK. Book recommendations, updates on stories, and snippets from works-in-progress—plus a free story in her Dancing Princesses world for signing up!

Available November 2023!

Sanctuary Hall — Finders & Binders book 1

Magic breeds misery

Augusta fails to hold her family together, despite her magical gift for binding. Her cracked world breaks wide open the day her father decides to declare her vanished mother dead. Retracing the steps her mother took before fleeing promises to heal Augusta . . . or reveal the wrongness at the heart of her magic.

Luella loves her home of farms and fields amid swamps—but her magic ensures she finds every lost thing. One too many careless words of items lost in the wrong place, and her clan elders send her off to learn to control her magic . . . except truly grasping her power requires giving up hope of returning home.

Cheng speaks to the air and the earth, and they reply, ensuring he never walks alone. Until the day his work on the railroad upsets the elemental balance within him—and bit by bit he loses the ability to communicate with other humans.

The pages of *Sanctuary Hall* practically turn themselves in a moving tale of people facing their worst enemy: their own magic.

Read on for a taste!

Augusta Deyo's world cracked wide open seven years after the first fissure.

The rupture started at the breakfast table, no less, right after she'd swallowed warm tea well-laced with clover honey. The comfortable clothes she'd donned earlier suddenly turned too tight, from her foundation garments to her starched ivory blouse. The little lace ruffle pinned at her throat pressed against her windpipe. Even the wide legs of her plum-colored linen skirt-pants seemed to wrap close around her skin. A thin layer of sweat slicked her bobbed curls against her skull, despite the early summer morning cool. Her whole body flushed to the point that her pale hands appeared ruddy against the fussy yellow-swirls-on-cream tablecloth.

Silence drowned all the usual sounds. No more chimes of silver-plated utensils against china or grunts as her father and brothers ate. No thumps overhead where the two-months-new hired help was making beds, or clanging from the cook-housekeeper back in the kitchen No rattle of wagons outside or calls from the newspaper girl parading down the street.

Even her own breathing stilled in her ears, though her throat and chest rose and fell against the taut fabric of her clothes. For that matter, everyone else in the room stopped moving and went quiet, the four of them unevenly spaced around the table that could fit twice as many with ease. The table that still had four empty chairs, including one at the foot, though no one had sat in them for years.

Seven years.

The room had barely changed a whit since then. The same yellow-and red-striped paper bedecked the walls. No one had moved the quiet landscape prints hanging at regular intervals around the room, save to dust the frames. The rectangular maple table rested atop the old woven-straw rug. The legs pressed against the exact same spots as they always had, the better to hide the worn holes revealed in the recent spring cleaning.

Had the world frozen? Albany was built on fixed land that moved only as allowed. The city had been solid for centuries, ever since the first Europeans came and bound the earth, or maybe even before when the Haudenosaunee and Mohican met and traded in the area.

Not even so much as a decorative boulder in the Capitol Park dared roll a meter or two without magical permission. All the bindings that kept the city running remained as they should be. No city in the Reconstituted Union of North America could claim more solid a foundation.

Only once had Augusta felt the least quiver of land energy, that day when something in her had connected with the deep earth and found flares of hot liquid beneath the bedrock. The merest drop of the flowing power had burned, offering a hard reminder that everything in the world could move, would move, *did* move, even if slower than humans noticed.

Everything moved sooner or later.

Everything changed.

Including her, whether or not she liked it.

Seven years ago, she'd hovered on the brink between girl and woman. She'd matured into a capable woman in her early twenties, trying to walk in her mother's footsteps and finding them—still—always—too big.

The lukewarm tea tasted of bile as she swallowed. Lifting a shaky hand to her throat, she tore open the lace ruffle. The small circle brooch that had kept it closed popped open, and the pin scratched but didn't draw blood.

The brooch slipped through her fingers and clattered as it came to rest against the edge of her plate. Sound and movement returned— wagon wheels rumbled outside, thuds overhead, and harsh breaths echoed around the table.

Across from Augusta, her older brother, Jacob Deyo crunched on a bite of buttered toast. He dropped the half-eaten crust onto his plate alongside congealing eggs of an appallingly cheery yellow. He had their father's solid build and dark-brown hair, gelled flat against his head, and wore a perfectly creased gray suit of summerweight wool with a wine-red tie in a loose bow and a matching handkerchief folded in the top right breast pocket. Yet the wide brown eyes in the stark, lean lines of his face spoke of their mother's blood.

Her father, Cornelius Deyo, wore a more sedate blue suit than his son in an older, classic cut, his collar and cuffs stark white against his ruddy-beige coloring. He folded his napkin and set it alongside his plate. The eggs and toast were scattered over the surface, hiding how much or little he'd eaten other than consuming all of his slices of bacon. The end of his long, thin nose twitched, but otherwise the muscles of his broad face were taut, and the white at his temples stark against his brown hair.

Only her youngest brother, Danny, continued to eat as though nothing had happened. His flat cap hung off one side of his chair, clean and neat but a bit battered and thus a good match for his shirt and breeches, the latter held up by blue suspenders. He slipped a sixth piece of bacon from the serving platter and munched on. His eyes—a lighter brown than father or brother—flashed Augusta's way to see if she'd make a fuss.

Not today, not with their father's words still echoing in her head.

Not when she still held hope she'd misheard him.

"Would you mind repeating that?" Jake—not Jakey anymore, even among family—raised his eyebrows as he leaned back in his chair, the wood creaking beneath him. He braced his hands against the edge of the table, fingers creasing the linen.

At least Augusta wasn't the only one taken aback. Small comfort, but she'd learned to take it where she could get it.

"It's been seven years since your mother left. There's been no sign of her since. No letters, no cards with blurry postmarks, not even any sightings in responses to the notices I placed in newspapers throughout the country." Father rubbed his forehead, gaze fixed on the table. "I wish this weren't so, but . . . under the circumstances, I'm petitioning to have her declared legally dead."

Danny hadn't seemed to pay attention, but he shot to his feet. His chair creaked and lurched back, nearly hitting the wall. Crumbs of bacon dropped from his clenched hands as he asked, voice high and tight, "Mama's dead? Frank and Callie, too? Cousin Nanette?"

"No, no." Their father rose, leaning over the table to take Danny's hands between his. "As far as I know they're all alive. But there's been no word of any of them. Or *from* them, and Frank and Callie are old enough they should remember our address and be able to send word."

Augusta ran a finger along the top of the empty chair next to her, where her younger sister had once sat. Another empty beyond it had been last used by their distant cousin Nanette. Across the way, Frank's chair sat empty between Jake and Danny, and their mother's at the foot of the table.

"They're not coming home? Ever?" Danny's round face looked older than his years, and for the first time his voice cracked.

"I don't know. I'll never stop looking for them, posting advertisements, paying investigators, searching for the kind of pathwalker who could locate them." Father squeezed Danny's hands, but his shoulder rounded and the lines of his face spoke of exhaustion. "Maybe someday . . ."

"But it's been years." Jake snatched a piece of bacon and crumbled it over his plate. "Anything could have happened." He leaned over to rub Danny's back. "We're still here, same as always. How much do you even remember Frank or Callie? You were little when they left."

"Frank used to get breezes to steal my toys and hide them up high, then Callie would get them back for me." Danny stuck his chin out. "It was a game between them. And Nanette sang me to sleep, never using words only *la la la*."

"It's just Mother who Father's asking to have declared dead." Augusta tried to smile at Danny as she forced the words out. "Seven the years to the day since she left. You couldn't wait another week or month or . . ." Her voice cracked too, and she swallowed hard.

Releasing November 2023!

ABOUT THE AUTHOR

Alea Henle writes non-fiction by day and fantasy by night. She's moved around a lot (had drivers' licenses from nine different states—one at a time!) and enjoys visiting new places and considering ways to incorporate them in her stories.

Be among the first to hear about new Twisting World tales—visit Alea's website (aleahenle.com) and sign up for her newsletter!

www.ingramcontent.com/pod-product-compliance
Lightning Source LLC
Chambersburg PA
CBHW061436210726
48287CB00007B/2235